Dying To Be Straight!

Michael D. Beckford

SpeakPublishing International
"Reeling in One Reader at a time."
www.speakpub.com

Like SpeakPublishing on Facebook
Follow SpeakPublishing on Twitter

Dying To Be Straight!
Michael D. Beckford

All the characters in this book are fictitious, and any resemblance to actual persons, living or dead is purely coincidental.

Copyright ©2011 by Michael D. Beckford. All rights reserved. No part of this book may be reproduced, scanned, downloaded, transmitted or stored in a retrieval system without the author or publisher's written consent.

ISBN-10: 0-9824189-7-3
ISBN-13: 978-0-9824189-7-0

SPEAKPUBLISHING BOOKS EDITION
Attention: Schools, Churches, Corporations and Non-Profit Businesses. SPEAKPUBLISHING books are available at quantity discounts with bulk purchase for educational, business, church or sales promotional use. For information please send an email to *michaeldbeckford@gmail.com* or *speakpubone@gmail.com* with subject: Bulk ordering, or call 407-470-4462.

Cover Photograph by: Yuri_Arcurs/Bigstock.com
Cover Design by: Wilken Tisdale III (cesear226@aol.com)
Back Cover Photograph by: Antareo Johnson
Public Relations Intern: Durdsny Nemorin (nemorinld@aol.com)
Public Relations Intern: Whitley Waymon
  (whitley1.waymon@gmail.com)
Public Relations: Renee (rw.jrconsulting@gmail.com)

First Printing September 2011
Third Edition September 2016

Visit our website at
www.speakpub.com

Dedication

We must all speak up against the demonic spirits of temptation, lust, fornication, adultery and homosexuality. This is rather a call for deliverance of all those brothers and sisters whom are facing the ugliness of sin and a testimony that you can overcome that questioning.

I dedicate this book to all whom have been lost in the struggle, you know who you are. To the ones whom have been bullied, ostracized, and made to seem like less than a person, I dedicate this book to you too. I also dedicate this book to all of the victims who suffered from rape, molestation, and abuse. I just want you to know that God hears your cries and He loves you too.

Praise For Dying To Be Straight!

"Just from the title of this book, I was dying to read it. I've read several books regarding homosexual lifestyles from the late E. Lynn Harris and a few other male authors, but Michael's approach was completely different. He basically took me on a journey from birth to the present day for his main character, Paul Stringer, and told the story from a first-person point-of-view so it was easy to follow. This was an emotionally compelling storyline told in less than 300 pages which made for a quick read. And I loved the author's usage of similes and metaphors throughout the book."
-Barbara Joe Williams
Author of 'A Man of My Own'

"This is great book and it's affordable! A book full of chapters to keep you wanting more! I finished the book in 3 days! I was great 2 see what men goes thru."
-Desjulmom 10

"I really enjoyed reading this novel. It was a great and easy read. Michael really hits home with his writing. In this one book it deals with so many issues. If you have any issues you can always look to Michaels books to uplift and open your eyes to a bunch of issues."
-Willette

More Praise For Dying To Be Straight!

"The author, Michael Beckford gives an inspiring narrative of a man trying to find himself and love on a self- destructive path that wasn't chosen by him. Many people have their assumptions about homosexual lifestyles but this book takes you deep into the mindset of someone who doesn't want to be gay.
The African-American community could benefit from the reading of this book. 'Dying to be straight' breaks down those barriers that sometimes cloud our mind and judgment when it comes to homosexuality."
-**Ashley Williams**
Contributing Writer of FAMU's Journey Magazine

"Dying" deals with some of the tough issues that most Christian writers would not tackle, but Beckford tackles them head on. Homosexuality, H.I.V., A.I.D.S., Sexual Abuse by Family, Acceptance from God."
-**The Oracle Magazine**
Theoraclemag.com

Acknowledgements

It absolutely takes a labor of love when writing a book. In the year of 2008 the Lord presented me with a vision to write this book, I was still dealing with some deliverance issues of my own and I certainly was not willing or enthusiastic to write a book such as this. I was ashamed because I was in constant fear of what my friends and family may think of me and what a book like this would do to my career as a writer. But little did I know, the God I serve is an awesome God; he told me that this book will be published at the age of twenty-six, the same age as my character Paul Stringer. And here I am three years later, finally with a finished product that I could be proud of. Although my personal story is in no way shape or form a resemblance of Paul Stringer, I did share with Paul's issue in combating the spirit of homosexuality which has run rampant in the lives of both the unsaved and the saved alike.

One thing I realize in this world is that people will judge you no matter how good or bad you are doing, that's just apart of the territory, but I come to tell you that there is freedom in sharing our pain with others, there is freedom in Christ and there is freedom in my life. As stated before, this book is certainly not about me, this book is about the millions of Americans and people of the world whom are struggling with a lifestyle of homosexuality.

I understand that the very words in this book can either make or break my career as a Christian writer, but that's ok, God has the final words in all things, and even if this is the last book I ever publish, at least I was obedient to His word and published this work of fiction.

I remember the first time I revealed the synopsis of this story to the gentleman in my former life-group (a group of Christian young men helping each other to become great). I felt so embarrassed and afraid of what they were going to say, but instead I was embraced, my hand was held in love and I felt more confident in the vision that God had given me in 2008.

There were so many people whom have impacted the development of this book it almost felt like a stage production. I definitely have put so much more energy into this book than previous books, not saying that the quality of the other books weren't up to par, but this book seemed to have taken a lot of my soul to produce. With every up there seemed to be a down and the enemy has been fighting hard for me to not be able to publish this work.

Many individuals don't understand the countless hours it takes for an author to craft a book. If I could turn in my time sheet now and the time sheet of others whom have been working and consulting with me on this project since 2008, I will surely have to turn in at least $300,000 worth of work, but many of us authors will never see that kind of money in return for our labor. Our books are worth more than the ninety nine cents a person pays for a single track of music, the people that are involved in every aspect is worth a lot more than that. But yet that's the price people expect for a book these days just because it is available on some sort of digital media. So I thank you, you the reader in advance who has bought this book in support of not only Michael Beckford, but the ministry and the people who have served to make this book a reality. Without you the reader, there simply will be no writers. Thank you. God bless you.

I give much thanks to my new manager Antareo Johnson, my brother; you are not only a creative genius, but you help to inspire me to push the envelope. You make sure I don't settle for less, you make sure whatever I am doing that it is the best. You are my prayer partner, my business partner and one of my closest friends. I thank you Antareo for all that you have done for me and Speak Publishing thus far. Thank you.

Demetrius Wilken Tisdale III, you have been with our company for a while, I am so privileged to see your growth as an artist. Demetrius, you are truly God sent, you don't complain, you just get the job done and keep it moving. You are a hero man; you are a hero to me because you have been such a blessing to Speak Publishing, I can't even thank you enough. I just pray that God continues to soar your skills as a graphic designer and congratulations once again with your position for the Journey Magazine.

Much love goes out to my Sonship Church family, before I began attending Sonship I laughed at people who spoke in tongues and my relationship with Jesus Christ was more on a business level than a personal level. I thank all of you for your indirect support of me and for being there when I was in trouble both spiritually, financially and in the natural. Thank you Pastor Susan and the rest of my church family, rest in peace brother Gary Huizenga, you gave what many couldn't give, and that was laughter to the weary and food to the needy.

I thank you Dawn Bruce for all the hard work and time that you gave to Speak Publishing. I just want you to know that your work was truly not in vain.

I thank you Durdsny Nemorin one of my newest public relations interns. I am so awe struck about her because she barely knew me; as a matter of fact I didn't even meet her until a few weeks after I learned about her working for SpeakPublishing. She caught the vision and has been excited to work. She is a blessing indeed, it's amazing how God can have people working on our behalf, good honest people that we never have met. So thank you Ms. D, I look forward to a great working relationship with you.

Many thanks also goes to Whitley Waymon, she has been very adamant in her pursuit to work with SpeakPublishing, and I appreciate her enthusiasm and many phone calls while earning her a position with our company.

I thank you Renee for the consulting you have been doing with us and giving our company the insight and lift we needed in terms of our public relations efforts. Thank you Renee and I look forward to our continued friendship.

I thank the members of the *Tallahassee Authors Network* specifically the founders Barbara Joe Williams and Marilynn Griffith, I appreciate the opportunity to share my talents with like minded individuals. You all are a great support group and remarkable writers as well.

I thank you Mom and Dad for your continued encouragement for me to do better and be better in my life. Every time I speak to you all I seem to get new motivation to complete my dreams and visions which God has given me. Thank you both for being there with me from the start, and when all else fails, all we have is family. Thank you.

I thank all friends, family and business partners which were not named, I certainly appreciate your contributions to my life and appreciate you too. God bless you.

Special Corporate Thanks:

I would like to thank one of my good friends in the publishing business Mrs. Cheryl Jennings of Sokhechapkepublishing Inc. She is an honest publisher based in the City Of Tallahassee and can be found at sokhechapkepublishing.com or by e-mail: info@sokhechapkepublishing.com

I give many thanks to my long time friend Joey Avilus for his continued support and giving me a job years ago with his company Discount Transportation LLC based in Tallahassee, Fl. There are a lot of college students in Tallahassee who lack transportation; my friend has been in busy for a while so I will advise anyone to call 850-264-3418.

Another one of my good friends, fellow co-workers and current barber is my friend Mahir Rutherford; he has been cutting my hair for at least three years. I'm so proud of him and Book opening up their new shop Kwik Kutz, they are also based in Tallahassee, Fl and can be reached at 850-219-0100.

I thank my good friend Napoleon Hinson who inspires me as a business owner to go the distance and to do better as an entrepreneur. His company specializes in selling detail supplies and janitorial products 850-251-5315. Thank you Napoleon for making this book possible.

Larry Hyler is more than a friend to me, he is like a father. I call him or he calls me at least once a day, he's one of my co-workers with ADT. He's a man of many words and much wisdom, he's been there to encourage me on days that I have been down and prayed with me at times I just needed to be lifted up. Thank you Larry for serving one of God's children, me. Larry currently works for ADT in Orlando, FL and can be reached at 850-294-5853. Thank you Larry and thank you to all of the individuals named an unnamed that has helped to show their support through encouragement, sponsorship and love in making this book possible. God Bless you.

Prologue: In the Club

Everybody in the club just do your thing, the D.J. spat in the mic. "Everybody in the club just do your thing," he repeated, while scratching a mix-tape version of 'Shake it all Night!' on the one's and two's, "Now rock, rock, rock with me. So shake, shake, shake what your mama gave ya!" The hyped-on-Hypnotic D.J. chanted. He quickly surveyed the room. "Hey you young honey back there," he announced, "come on up to the D. J. booth," pointing his mic toward someone in the back corner of the dance club "Yeah, you in the yellow tight pants. Girl you got a booty that will make you say Jesus!"

The yellow-tight-pants girl emerged from the darkness. The purple, red, and blue silk waist-tie shirt hugged her slender torso and exposed her bare back. Soft, creamy, and chocolate, she continued to make her way through the crowd, placing her blue suede gladiator stilettos firmly one in front of the other. Her killer runway walk caught the attention of several onlookers.

"Yeah you, come on up. Why you acting like you scared? You got all those men drooling and waiting in line to get behind you." Men silently nodded in agreement. A few cat calls were heard in the distance. "You might as well come on up and show everybody what you got."

"That's it baby girl, you doing it, come on up a little more." Once in the spotlight with the D.J., it was easier to make out the girl's facial features and silhouette. The D.J., on the other hand, looked raunchy in comparison. "Girl, God made Eve for Adam, but He sho'nuff' made you for me. Sister girl, what's your name? Where you from? And you don't even have to tell me who you with."

"First of all, my name is Kesha," the girl finally said, shifting her weight from one leg to the other, "and I'm from the 305, and I'm just kicking it with my home girls, picking up a few drinks and just having a little fun. We just want to bring in the New Year right."

"Ok, ok, do you have a man?" The D.J. asked.

"No, I don't have a man, but I have men friends." Kesha looked at the D.J. with a sly smile.

"Can I be your friend baby?" He licked his lips, nearly touching the tip of the microphone.

"Sure, you can be my friend. You got some cheese for me D.J.?"

"Oh, ok, so you high maintenance?" He looked at Kesha as if she was crazy for mentioning money.

"Of course," she swooshed her hair to one side, "I don't have a real big booty for nothing. I am a *for profit* business," Kesha said, placing her hands on her hips. Again, she shifted her weight in her stilettoes. "I don't mess with no dudes unless he taking care of me. Shoot, I work off of salary plus commission." Kesha exaggerated with a wink.

"Ok, ok, you have said it all. Ladies and gentleman, I'm going to bring you back some of the hottest music. In the meantime, me and home girl gone talk a little."

The D.J. pulled Kesha to the side. "So, what's up? I got a hotel ready for you tonight. You down?"

"Heck no! I don't even know you dude." Kesha balled up her fingers.

"But, but," he began to stutter, "I can make all your dreams come true."

"Can you really do that? Do you really even know me?"

"I know that you got a big butt and had a bunch of guys lined up to be with you."

"Yeah, and so what?" Kesha lashed back.

"*So what?* Then you must be doing something right. I can hardly get a guy to be with me if my life depended on it," the D.J. said, admiring Kesha's physique" I play at Club G like every other weekend, and I'll be lucky to get looks."

"Maybe you in the wrong spot then, maybe you should be down there with the people," Kesha gestured "But since you sound so sad, I'll be at your hotel at like two o'clock."

"Sweet, I'll check you later." He smirked back at Kesha.

He couldn't wait to get to the hotel to do every evil that crossed his mind.

Welcome to the underground life of dudes with dudes and girls with girls. The dudes hang out at Club G, which is short for Gomorrah, and the females hang out at club S, short for Sodom. My name is Kesha, and my name is also Paul. By day I am a fully educated black male with a B.S. Degree in Science. By night, my name is Kesha, and if ever a dude is into finding hot guys, his best bet is to go to Club G.

Yes, I was born a guy, but for some reason, I picked up female tendencies along the way. This is not the way I was born, and ultimately not the way I want to be. I am dying for my freedom, and dying to be straight. And oh, that D.J. at the club is Jesse, one of the biggest faggots around this town. I can't talk about him much because, well, it's so complex. Last night wasn't the first time I met him, and neither will it be the last.

Like I said before, my name is Paul, I'm twenty-six years old at the time of writing this, and this is my story.

Part 1

"*And likewise also the men, leaving the natural use of the woman, burned in their lust one toward another; men with men working that which is unseemly, and receiving in themselves that recompence of their error which was meet.*"
Romans 1:27 K.J.V.

Welcome to Our World Paul

On May 1, 1984 I was born to Will and Alicia Stringer. My parents said that I weighed about three pounds and three ounces. The room was morbid, painted with a jailbreak white and windowless at the same time, as my parents described to me in years past. Although the culture of the room was not surprising for a hospital, my mother took a candle and set it near her bedside to represent the first year of my birth. My father blew the candle when I first arrived out of the womb of my mother as the doctor and nurses gazed on with glee. My dad said he was so proud to see me born. There I was in the doctor's hands, naked, a little bit of hair on my head, and yes, *a boy*. In fancier terms, we scientist love to call it, the 'xy' chromosome. At the time of my birth, I knew nothing of my nakedness; all I knew to do was cry for attention. The doctor had already cut my umbilical cord, and there I was surrounded by my parents and their good friends.

The doctor washed me up, and then covered me up in a little blue gown, and then the doctor passed me around like a Thanksgiving turkey. Everyone, of course, gave their oohs and ahhs... and I just wanted to sleep. My mom said that all of the joy of the world was bundled into me. I was the first of five children.

One year passed from the day of my birth and my mom and dad were at it again, laughing, crying, and of course, passing me around like a hot turkey. This time, all the friends and neighbors were there to witness the first birthday of little Paul. Of course, I did not know who all these people were. They all looked like aliens to me. There I was talking my gibberish language, and all of them were actually speaking English. I wasn't a good little baby that stayed quiet most of the time. No, I gave my parents hell, and cried and cried till the cake got cut. I even wet my pants. I wanted all the attention, not realizing at the time that I did have all the attention. My parents knew right then at my first birthday that I would be someone special, and that I would be quite a load on their hands.

My first full year was like my best year, because I was able to do everything I wanted without getting spanked. I would pick up the toys from the floor and put them in my mouth. I would pull on my mom's rug, use the bathroom in the living room, dining room and kitchen. Hey, I guess I was in baby heaven. Every time my mom wanted to spank me, my dad would say, "Wait a little longer, He doesn't know any better. Just give him some time; he'll come around." Yeah right. I would cry and scream when I didn't get my way, especially when I was missing the warm milk from my mother's breast. Every moment of that first year was a pretty sweet deal for me.

What maybe sweet for one person may not be sweet for others. Approaching my terrible two's, I could remember my mom constantly saying, "Lay the rod and spare the child." She was laying that rod alright, and of course I was the child. My mother would keep me in my place, and I quickly learned what it meant to be potty trained. No more peeing in the kitchen, and definitely no more peeing on her good couch in the living room. Mom was getting fed up with me, and daddy was tired of hearing her complaints. So, being the father he was, he started laying the rod, too. I was no longer a turkey, but a roasted ham cut up in tiny cubes. You can say it was discipline, I would say it was discipline, either way, I learned my young life lessons as I was two months shy of two years old.

As a little baby, you barely know what everything was for. As a matter of fact, you pretty much know nothing. All you know to say is mama and dada and hope for the best that they'll hear you and be there to take care of you. My parents were my first line of defense; otherwise, I was helpless.

Of course at the time I knew nothing of what it meant to be a Stringer. My family is a very affluent family. My dad is a chemist, and my mother is a big time lawyer. At two years of age, all I knew was what was presented to me, and that was two loving people who gave me life, love, and a dream to be like the big kids.

Bad Uncle

I think I was like four or five when both of my parents began to get really busy. My mother decided to go back to work and pursue her career as a top attorney, and my dad also became much busier. Eventually, "Who is going to watch Paul?" became the question-of the-day rerun. During the day time, I was in daycare, but finding someone to supervise me at night while my parents worked overtime was often the problem. My mother had to work anywhere between seven, nine and ten at night on a case. At that time, my mother was trying to make partner at the Reardon&White law firm, one of the most prestigious law firms in Miami. And she was doing all that she could to make partner in a years time. My dad, on the other hand, didn't begin work until two in the afternoon. He usually didn't get home from his job until about ten or twelve at night. While my parents weren't home, that left me to be looked after.

Like I said, I was four or five years old at the time, and I was fully able to speak my broken English, and I even knew all my ABC's and more. At that age, I had a good idea of what was right or wrong, and hot or cold. My parents taught me well. Often times due to my parents' absence, I had to stay with my aunt and uncle, who weren't the nicest relatives to be with. But they kept me night in and night out, as my parents strived to further their careers and make a better life for me.

One winter night in October, I was misbehaving, and there was no food at my aunt and uncle's house, so that made me become even more rambunctious. My aunt finally made the decision to pick up a few edible goods from the grocery store. It was the first time that I was left alone with my uncle, and I continued to play in the back room, you know, being loud and doing kid's stuff. Moreover, I was disturbing him from watching his football game. So he came back there and told me to be quiet or else.

"Or else what?" I inquired, in a way that only a four or five year old would say. So he got mad at me for back talking him and he immediately pulled down his pants. He commanded that I touch it; I was very hesitant. Then he loosened his belt buckle and yelled at me.

"Touch it!" he said again. Then, I quickly did what was commanded of me, but started to pull my hand back when he pulled my body closer to his and started to touch my penis.

I didn't know what was going on, or why it was happening. I felt like I was in a trance. He let me go after about a minute of fondling and pointed at his penis and said, "This right here is the law and no one tells it what to do."

So there I was in grave shock, in amazement, wondering what just happened to me. As he and I heard the front door crack open, he hurried and whispered in my ear.

"If you tell anybody, I will send you to the psych ward."

It was too late, though. The seed was already planted, but I didn't tell anyone for a good year or so. When my parents picked me up from my aunt and uncle's house, I couldn't say anything. I was mute as a squirrel, wouldn't speak to anyone. All I could do was shake my head yes or no when spoken to, never ever giving a verbal response.

I kept to myself the rest of that year, talking to no one, still thinking about what my uncle said and trying to figure out why it had to happen to me. Every time I went over my aunt and uncle's house, I cried and cried, but wouldn't say a word. And yes, that little incident with my uncle and me happened at least ten more times. And there he was steady threatening me, as he abused me, sat me in his lap and pulled my pants down while he masturbated. I hated it. I really, really hated it, but after the eighth time, I started thinking what my uncle was doing to me was alright.

I started thinking that everyone's uncle masturbated while they sat in his lap; maybe it was normal.

My mother was working on having me a little brother while all the stuff was going on with me and my uncle. She barely noticed me, and all my pops knew was that I was going through changes. Well, I was going through changes alright. I was changing into something I never asked to be. I was changing into a monster, something with a hunger and lust for men my uncle's age, thinking that it was proper and right for me to sit in their laps so they can get *happy*.

Finally, my auntie started noticing some strange things not only in me, but also in my uncle, especially. She noticed that he spent fewer nights wanting to have sex with her, and she also noticed that his pants were always wet when I was around. So, one day my aunt told her husband that she was going to the store. She drove off about two blocks down the street so he wouldn't see her car, and she walked back to the house to see what was really going on.

My aunt peeked through the window to the back room where she usually left me playing with my toys while my uncle sat in the living room watching football. That day when my aunt peered in, she saw me, and she saw my uncle. I was sitting in my uncle's lap, helping him to get happy. I was happy, too, because I started to like it. My auntie rushed around the house and through the front door. She said she couldn't believe her God-given eyes. My uncle jumped up hysterically and pushed me off of him, and my aunt just stared at us both in the back room teary eyes. Her worst fears were staring right at her, and silence said everything. She grabbed my little arms, pants sagging halfway down my thighs, and pulled the door as we went running to the car. All the while she was screaming out all kinds of slurs, as she raced me to my mom's office.

My aunt attempted to explain all that she had witnessed to my mother, but to no avail. My mother looked up at me as perplexed as a hound dog, asked the simple question, "of what's going on, Paul?"

Then and right then I broke my silence and said, "My uncle told me to make him *happy*."

She said, "What do you mean make him happy and why are your pants undone?"

My aunt interjected and said, "The boy was being fondled by my husband, and no telling what else happened."

"Oh my God, oh my God," my mother exclaimed, and she began to fall backwards. Luckily, my aunt was strong enough to catch her and hold her up, or my brother, who was in her stomach at the time, might not have been born. My mother got up, got on the phone and called my father. He left his job immediately and headed over my aunt and uncle's house. My mother felt we needed to get over there quickly before my father killed his brother.

My father didn't kill his brother, but he surely put him in the hospital for a week. I, on the other hand, was put under an evaluation by a psychologist until I turned six. All I could hear for a year was my mother and father apologizing for not paying closer attention to me. They were extremely sorry for what my uncle did to me. And because my mother had my brother when I was five, she didn't make partner. She made the wise decision to stay home and raise my brother Luke and I. My mother promised that I and my brothers would never have to go through what I went through ever again. So she made a conscious decision to home school us. Although everything my parents did for me at the time was all good and well, needless to say it was too late for me. I couldn't stand the pressure and infinite thoughts of being with another man. At this point in my life, my body was saying that I was a guy, but my hormones were saying otherwise. Who would have known that the scars put on me from my uncle would affect me all the way up until now. I personally felt like I was pushed into a lifestyle of homosexuality because the decision surely was not mine. All I knew at the age of six was that change was on the way for me, but it was hard for me to accept it.

Changes

Some change the physical, some change the mental, I, on the other hand, pretty much changed both. By the innocent age of ten, I began a small tendency to twist like a girl, my voice also screeched a little and I was very fearful of guys my age. Every chance I could get, I would lay my eyes on one of the grown male teachers, just to see if I could get a peek of his muscular build. Oops. My bad. I forgot to tell you that my mom gave up home schooling and allowed me to go to public school.

My brother was four when I started going to school by myself, and he carefully started figuring out that there was something wrong with me. I didn't really notice the differences at the time. I felt modestly normal and shy for the most part. Yes, the girls looked good in the fourth grade, but they seemed to complain a lot, and be too much of a responsibility. Guys were cool, calm, and collective, didn't care about breaking a nail, and could care less about peeing behind a tree. That carefree attitude is what attracted me to them, because girls just seemed too complicated.

While most kids were just learning about different body parts, I knew mine backwards and forwards. I even knew about that special spot where babies were formed. I knew all there was to know about a guy, but very little about a girl. Some say it was coincidence while others may say it was just my luck. I said that I could care less about most of what the others in school would say because I knew what I really wanted, and that was a chance to be made *happy*. I wanted my uncle. I don't know why. I knew it may have sounded crazy, but at the time, he seemed to be the only one who would be able to give me the attention that I needed.

Let's just say that the thought of wanting my uncle was as much a fantasy as any other fantasy I had in my life at the time. My uncle had been long kicked out my aunt's house, and I heard that he moved to Kansas. I wondered if there were other men to make my uncle happy in Kansas, too. Well, I haven't heard from him since his exodus.

So what was I to do? I was a simple little boy with adult dreams and fantasies attending elementary school. I did what a little boy my age would do. I would act out in class. Yep, that was my way of getting attention. My parents loved me dearly, but things weren't the same since the molestation occurred, they tried to be overprotective but it just kind of made things worst for me, I experienced some things at the age of four and five that no kid should have ever had to deal with. Quite frankly, my parents did not know how to deal with the problem. They saw the changes in me, but refused to acknowledge them.

So, there I was again. I felt mute and solitary in my own home. Sometimes I questioned my very existence.

Most of the time, my mother would say it's going to be alright, while my dad always relentlessly asked if I had a girlfriend yet. *As if having a girlfriend was going to change the way I felt about men.*

Twisted, tempered, and full of torment, I ran away. I ran away to find a place where I could be cool and accepted. Somewhere it was normal for guys to like guys and for girls to like girls. On my road trip, I traveled by bus as far as Orlando from Miami, my starting point for Kansas, thinking that Kansas was the missing link to my sexual and mental frustrations.

My parents were mad at me for months, and my mother threatened to home school me again. I promised her good behavior, so she allowed me to stay in public school.

During those days in school, being gay wasn't as popular as it is now. Nowadays, to be gay is like making a fashion statement, while sleeping with the same sex is just the icing on the cake. I, on the other hand, chose not to let anyone in on my secret, so I decided to behave as normal as possible. Sometimes trying to be what you're not has its many consequences. Kind of like the times when I was over aggressive with this girl in middle school. I, quote, "accidentally," un-quote, touched her on the butt. Of course I'm not proud of the many accidental moments, but they did give me the attention that I was looking for.

Matriculating from fourth grade to fifth grade was a true challenge for me. All I could think about at the time was the fifth grade prom coming up at the end of my fifth grade year. Every fourth grader in my class was talking about this big event. While I was dreading the very verb that the event placed in my mind, I didn't fully ignore it. My heart was broken, shattered, and confused because on one hand I wanted to dance with a well-dressed guy, on the other hand I knew that it was not permissible, and then again, I did not know of any guys at the school who were like me.

Yes, there were the rumors about the other guys, and yes I had my nose into everyone's business, but the end result always seemed to come up negative. At the dawn of my fourth grade year, everyone was all so interested in who was going with whom to the fifth grade prom. So one of the nicest girls in my fourth grade reading class came up to me and said, "Hey Paul, who you going to the dance with?" I stuttered and stared at her like she asked me what the capital of Idaho was.

Finally catching my breath I inquired, "Who needs to know?"

"Of course me silly," she giggled. When I asked her why, she said, "Just curious because you look lonely." I was young and naïve. I had no idea that this nice, giggly girl was asking me out to the fifth grade prom.

    I must confess, not only was she one of the nicest girls in school, but she was also one of the prettiest, too. Her name was Sandra Lopez. She was mixed with black and Hispanic. She had long silky hair, her eyes looked like glazed sparkling glass, teeth were white as snow complemented with a coke shaped body. Feeling like the dummy I was, I told Sandra that I'd get back to her and that I needed to ask my dad about it.

    The way she looked at me after I said I had to ask my dad about it would have made anyone think that I was a Vietnam Veteran who'd come back from war with one arm and one leg. The girl stared at me with a look of total disgust. Feeling the pressure within me to reconcile, I finally came to a peaceful resolution. I told Sandra that I'd be happy to take her to the fifth grade prom.

    If there was anything that I learned to be in my fourth grade year, was to be quick on my feet. And I must say, the next day when I officially accepted Sandra's offer, my popularity rating went off the charts. I was a hero, a popular young man, and I was gay. There I was playing Russian Roulette with my life, because I began to live deeper and deeper in a lie, for a life that everyone else wanted for me. Now I was confident that I was behind enemy lines, and it was too late to turn around.

Welcome to the 5th Grade Prom

As exciting as my fourth grade year was, it surely couldn't match the fantasy of my fifth grade year. All of my classmates were looking forward to the many fifth-grade trips. Fifth-grade field trips were the trips most anyone would kill to relive. Moments at the Space Camp, Henry Ford Museum and aquarium were all staples my classmates looked forward to and enjoyed. Well, not me. My fifth grade year was one of my most dreadful years, right along with my senior year at prom, but I'll talk about the infamous prom that took place seven years later-- later.

Fifth grade year, which in my opinion is the Holy Grail for snotty-nosed kids, geeks, gimmicks and talent shows, a time when all of us felt like somebody because we were finally the big dogs on campus. Many of the kids wore a countenance of pure pride, some with envy, while most with joy because they knew that middle school was soon coming. At the time, I didn't know how to tame this overwhelming cycle of pride and bliss. My mom was six months into yet another pregnancy, and I was lost in my insecurities while my younger siblings searched to find me. They did not understand the true complexity of what had happened to me, so they didn't really know me, they just knew of me. Sometimes I felt like a stranger in my own home, an outcast of sorts.

Accepting Sandra Lopez's invitation to the big dance was more than a spectacle for me that year; it was a lifestyle shift. *I didn't know that I was supposed to be her boyfriend, too.* Yes, I was forced yet again to be someone's play toy, and in many ways I wasn't happy about it. Many times I would cry myself to sleep at night, asking God why I couldn't just be normal. During my cries, the most I heard from God was the tears wetting my pillow. And as I listened to the constant gay bashing through the news and saw the exhaustive teasing by fellow classmates toward boys with feminine tendencies, I was under the sincere impression that God hated me because of who I really was.

Needless to say, now I know better. I know that God never hated me. He's always loved me; he just hated the sin that lived inside of me. The pressure to get rid of that one specific sin--was always on my mind.

Many times Sandra and I would roam around the hallways, hands tied together; we looked like the perfect couple. I also felt like the perfect liar. Sandra often asked me what was wrong, because she could obviously sense that my demeanor was not quite right. She even eluded me about sex. I would have never guessed that sex was a physical activity that fifth graders pontificated. These brave youngsters even dared let the three-letter word roll off their tongues. I couldn't comprehend this in the world of coodies, farts and snotty-nosed girls. As she continued to question me, I continued to brush her off and denied that there was anything wrong. I was so ready to give Sandra the pink slip, but as I said before, I dug a hole so deep, that even Miami-Dade Fire Rescue would have a hard time digging me out of it.

As time continued to progress toward our fifth grade prom, I started getting used to Sandra, and I actually began to like the daily walks we shared around the school, basically announcing to all in our path that we were a legitimate couple. We often exchanged little pecks on the cheeks, and it sort of became more of a hobby than an emotional fulfillment for me. Sandra was the exact recipe I needed for the constant hunger for attention.

Unfortunately, while I thought that Sandra and my daily ritual was a hobby, she saw it as a bright spot to escalate our relationship to a new level. A level that involved kissing each other on the lips. She also came over to my house from time to time to watch Cartoon Network and Nickelodeon while we ate tuna fish sandwiches together. My mother and father were so overly happy for us, especially for me, that they didn't care about what else we could have done when they were gone. Not that I was looking forward to hitting a homerun, going to third base, or doing anything else that people talked in code about.

Only two weeks stood between me and the approaching big dance. By day fourteen, the entire fifth grade body was rocking in anticipation of this one curiously special night. I, on the other hand, couldn't wait for the credits to roll. While everyone else was counting down the days to the affair, I was counting down the days to its culmination. By day seven, everyone knew who was taking—or dragging—who to the dance, and who had no date at all. For the dudes who didn't have a girl to be with, I so badly wanted to say hey, here's one, she's available now. But I knew deep in my heart that I could not do that. I couldn't break the sensitive heart of the first girl who actually meant more than words could describe, just because she was the filler I needed to feel a hint of normalcy. On day two, as I held on to my sanity and still gained the respect I deserved, I had one more sizing for the tux I was going to wear. The crushing thoughts crossed my mind while I was being fitted. *Would the seamstress stab me with the safety pin? Was my uncle okay in Kansas? Would Sandra try to pressure me to have sex with her and if I gave in would I be cured?*

It's amazing how everything was happening because my mother was in labor while having my little brother Luke. Luke was being as rebellious as ever, and I was having the pain of my life with battling the truth.

The big night had finally arrived and it surely was no turning back. Walking into the overly decorated school cafeteria, I had seen a dashingly amazing Sandra staring at me with eyes of wolves, ready to devour me with her love. At that semi-awkward moment I had a peculiar heartbeat. Honest to God. I felt a tingling sensation rush down the lower extremities of my body. It was the answer to my prayer, the first time I felt an abhorrent sexual feeling for a girl. A feeling that felt to me to be so unnatural, but I knew it had to be right. I never realized that a 10-year-old, fifth-grade girl could have that much décolleté and a curiously curvy silhouette.

As Sandra walked toward me, and I walked toward her, my pants suddenly took on marching orders, and the immaturity of my masculinity had finally arisen to the beauty of Eve's ancestry. Wow, the wonders and joy it could be if only we started dancing, which we did. Dancing we'd begun, and I was highly embarrassed by what she told me was going on. After the discontent and embarrassment, my one piece wonder went like Humpty Dumpty and had a great fall. So then Sandra strapped her arms around me and I propped my hands on her waist.

I felt such a peace from the transaction of emotions that were taking place between Sandra and me that I didn't want the credits to roll anytime soon. All I wanted was one wish, and that wish was for that night to never end.

Of course, like all good things must, the night did end, but not before Sandra and I were named prom King and Queen. When my parents heard about it, they were delirious. They could not believe it. I could not believe it, either. I didn't want to believe it, but yes, it happened. My fifth grade class had spoken, and I have the pictures to prove it. While the hype about prom King and Queen preoccupied the minds of my classmates and dirty gossip rumors about prom-night hook-ups filled the mouths of babes, I was asking myself was I really normal or was the prom night jaunt just a spur of the moment ordeal. A hormonal fluke or maybe just an accident.

Night after night, our phone was ringing off the hook. People were calling left and right, congratulating me on procuring the fifth-grade throne. You would have thought that I was the first black President of the United States with all the press and attention I was receiving from the school newsletter. Although it was victorious for me, and indeed a moment of triumph, the questioning of my identity by me was now the number one topic on my daily, mental agenda.

As the weather man takes his pen and a map and forecasts clear skies, rainy days and dark nights, so did the forecast of my life become so dark while entering middle school.

Hit or Miss

I'm *choking. I said I'm choking,* is what I told one of the eighth-grade bullies.

He said, "Shut up you punk and give me all your lunch money." I gave it to him, feeling helpless and defeated. I no longer was the one who was top of the class; I was now the fish swimming at the bottom of the ocean. I told Sandra about it later on that day since the both of us went to the same middle school and all.

Sandra said one thing to me, "How come you gave it up."

"Gave what up?" I quickly replied.

"Your money?" She looked at me with a hollow expression.

I said, "Because I couldn't breathe, b...", I cussed her, and she was angry with me for the whole week.

As I reminisced on what happened that day, I started to think how defenseless I felt. It was a familiar feeling. I felt the way I did the day my uncle took something away from me, which was my pride and innocence. I gave it up. This bully barely took away my lunch money, but it felt like he took more. Thoughts started running through my mind; I was questioning myself once more, saying to myself that maybe *I am a punk*. Maybe that's what everyone saw me as, but I was too busy being a class clown, I never stopped to see what people really thought of me. That's probably why almost everyone in my entire family called me the week of my fifth-grade prom. They wanted to congratulate me because they no longer had to deal with having a *punk* in their family.

I didn't really know at the time if everyone thought I was a punk, and didn't really care to a certain degree, but I was concerned about how my girlfriend Sandra felt about me.

One thing that I've learned from the first serious conversation with my girlfriend was either girls could bring me real high like a perfect euphoria, or they could bring me real low like a train wreck from hell. Although Sandra was really mad at me, she decided to put me real high, and said nothing but good things to me, the perfect euphoria was working and my hormones for her were becoming even more evident. I mean, very evident.

So, later—when we finished conversing-- we did it. Yes. We did it. We did the rumble in the jungle and much more. I was so proud of myself that I went home crying. I was crying and professing in the streets, thought quite silently, that I was not gay anymore. I was so happy that I almost was run over by a car, a red Honda, which came a hair's width to killing me. I didn't even care, though, because I felt at least I was going to heaven now because I was in bed with a girl. When I arrived home that day, my entire family studied me with eyes mirroring that of a fresh sunrise. They questioned and questioned my whereabouts. I didn't budge. Didn't speak one word. I just went straight to the shower like a cheating husband.

    Of course my mom knew something was up. She didn't quite know what it was, so, following her motherly intuition, she decided to call Sandra on the phone. I was in the shower so I had no idea how the conversation unfolded. It wasn't until later, once I was out the shower, that I learned that Mom went behind my back and called my girlfriend to get the skinny on me. All my mother told me was that Sandra was giggling hysterically over the phone like a one-year-old.

    I surely did not want to give up the information about the moment that Sandra and I had, especially since I was sworn to secrecy; I said nothing.

    "You know, Paul, you can tell your mother if you and Sandra are having sexual relations. Your father and I won't punish you." My mother said light heartedly. She was trying so hard to get something out of me from that moment on for a whole month. In the meantime, I was beginning to change, my life was beginning to blossom faster than a butterfly stays in cocoon. My life, as I knew it, was beginning to come out of the closet.

    Yes, the days of intimacy and pleasure with Sandra were good, but I wanted more. I wanted everything that I could have ever fantasized and dreamed about. And those dreams were purely to be with a tall, sexy, handsome man. Not only did he have to be big and strong in the abs and arms, but also in places I'd rather not talk about. He had to be almost a standing replica of my uncle. Needless to say, those fantasies I had, I didn't realize how soon they would come true.

Sandra was one of the first to notice a difference in me. I wasn't giving my all when we were making love in the sixth grade, and most importantly I was holding back my true feelings, cravings and desires. It was driving her *crazy*.

How can I, a teenage male, tell my female counterpart that I was in lust after a guy; a guy who was in the eighth grade, a guy whose name was simply Brian.

Throughout my sixth grade tenure, Sandra argued back and forth with me about my loving her. I told her it was simple, "I love you, but I'm also falling in love with another man." The girl almost had a heart attack. Question after question she asked me, and I broke down and told her the whole truth, nothing but the truth. She felt so ashamed, so embarrassed that the guy she loved was in love with another guy.

Looking back at that moment, I think I used the word *love* quite loosely because I barely knew Brian, but I did know two things, he was black and he was gay. Sandra was so hurt, and I was hurt too because I felt that I let her down. I felt like I betrayed her. But most importantly, I felt free because finally after two years of silence, I was able to tell her the truth. Consequently, the two of us broke up, and she promised me to keep our secret in perfect peace.

So, I began to pursue Brian. That's when he noticed me.

I'm in Love with Brian

Brian Macon was at the top of his class in Webb Middle School. The dude was an *A* average student, and a celebrity basketball player for the school as well, but many didn't know he had a secret. I, too, was shocked to learn his secret because he always surrounded himself with plenty of girls. He was tall, handsome, and always had the latest, trendiest haircut. The boy looked good enough to be in GQ magazine. I mean he was quite the stud.

After one of our home court games, I simply looked in his eyes and asked him if he was down. He twitched his eyes to the left and to the right, and made a fuss about what I was talking to him. At that moment I felt like something was probably up, because most people with his stature would have tried to beat me up, flush my head in the toilet, sabotage my belongings, verbally humiliate me or something else just as crazy, but he simply said no. Of course I wasn't content with that answer, but I let it go anyway. I figured I'll ask him at a time when I can get him alone with no distractions, and when no one but me could hear his answer.

It was two o' clock p.m. Brian's physical education class had ended. I memorized his entire schedule, so I knew I had at least five minutes to speak with him before the last period. As I scurried across the gym, there he stood, sweating at attention. I just wanted to grab him and tell him all my thoughts about him. But no, I stood my ground and asked him the question again. As the last syllable of the last word I spoke echoed through the gym, he flinched. Paused. A couple of seconds ticked by. He slowly opened his mouth. His eyes took inventory of the gym, as if to make sure he wasn't on Candid Camera. Then, his solid brown eyes found mine again and he uttered something. I couldn't make out what he said. So I waited for him to repeat his response. He didn't.

"Are you down?" I asked again. I stared him squarely in his eyes. Though, my eyes wanted to behold all of him. It almost pained me to remain poised. But, now I was running out of minutes. It would be time for the last period of the day soon. I needed him to repeat his response. ASAP. His returning glare was paralyzing. I thought this time for sure he was going to punch me in the face for asking him the same question again. I should have paid closer attention to him the first time. How foolish of me. Time was of the essence. He stepped an inch closer, my heart palpitating. Slowly, he opened his mouth. I yearned for him, for his round, plump lips. Juicy. But I had to compose myself. It was not the time for me to indulge in one of my illicit fantasies. He was about to speak. This time I heard him clearly.

"Y. E. S.", he spelled.

Yes, he was down. I didn't know whether to do a cheer or sprint to the other side of the full-court gym. All I knew was that it was good news for me and my unnatural fantasies.

Living in a fantasy world I thought some of the most foul of thoughts and pictured Brian in ways which girls probably didn't dream to think about him. I was in love with Brian, and I was shocked. Most importantly, he was like me--a gay freak.

Before leaving the gym, I retrieved Brian's phone number. Then, I walked out the front as he walked out the back of the gym. We both agreed that it was best that we did not see each other during school hours. Brian was such a modest and humble guy; just being in his presence aroused me. I wasn't one for getting all excited too quickly, but this guy, oh this guy; he cut the cake for me.

Many people took Sandra and my break up pretty hard. I, for one, found it very tough because I really did like the moments of intimacy we shared together. There was always something about Sandra that had made me till this day think twice about being gay. Some would say that the mere fact that she's a woman should be that particular *something*. That's true and all, but there's something else about Sandra that I'm still trying to figure out. Most people ask me now, how could a guy leave such a beautiful girl to be with another man? I tell them the answer is simple, abuse by my uncle and uncontrollable thoughts and imaginations which weigh heavily toward men.

Brian pretty much felt the same way I felt about things. The girls he had had sex with, he told me, and he just slept with them for status, not pleasure. Brian poetically told me this. To garner the pleasure, is to be able to complete your dreams and fantasies through the actual intervention of a partner. And that partner was me.

I was the one who made Brian happy when he was lonely; I was the one who he cuddled up with after a game. I was the one who he made love to for real, me. Yes, me. Paul Stringer was the man of his many dreams.

Hangin' Out

How can we feel both in love and lonely at the same time? Well I did my seventh-grade year in middle school. Brian had matriculated to high school. I had to suffer without the comfort of his presence. Like a mountain standing high above the clouds, so was the feelings of loneliness I felt in the seventh grade. The feeling of being caught by my peers and the pressure of being gay was all enough to make me feel like Dorothy from the *Wizard of Oz*. All I ever thought about throughout the school day was getting home, spending time with Brian. If only I had some red heels on my feet to click when I felt lonely, I would be invulnerable.

There weren't many climatic occasions to my seventh grade year, just a few noticeable changes that I didn't even notice, at least not at first. There were changes in the way I walked, changes in the way I talked, the ways of homosexuality were placing me in a state of an unfamiliar metamorphosis. Things were happening to me that I could not quite understand or even care to grasp.

That year was filled with the same ole' stuff, while Sandra filled me in with the evil eye as we passed by each other in the hallway. I knew in my heart, though, that there was no turning back for me, because all I knew was that I had a thing for men. A thing that almost cost me my life that year.

If I were to look at what people would call a normal relationship, the kind between a man and a woman, I would say that in a normal relationship the man is faithful to the woman only about fifty percent of the time. In an abnormal relationship, the kind between Brian and me, I would say that a man is faithful to a man about thirty percent of the time.

I think being a homosexual opens up the door to massive swinging, if that's' even the term to describe it. Some of my past boyfriends would probably say that I'm wrong. When Brian left for high school, I started seeing him less, and we practically stopped hanging out. I don't know if he started seeing another man, but I wasn't' about to crave somebody and not have him. So, I did what any guy would do; I started prospecting.

I started looking for something, someone, who would settle my urges for the time being, and I decided to do a little shopping for something sexy. I thought maybe Brian would start back noticing me if I boosted up my looks. Speaking of my looks, many times walking through those school doors, I felt the shame of evilness; therefore, I carried the shame of my sins on my face.

Sin. You may ask, why sin? Deep—deep, deep--down inside I felt that something was not right with what I was doing, but surely nothing could stop me, not then. No one except Richard Red. Richard Red almost killed me, literally.

I was in desperate need for attention and a new boyfriend; I cornered then fellow seventh grader Richard Red. I mean, he walked like a fagot, talked like a fagot, so I approached him to see if he truly was. I kind of approached him the same way that I approached Brian. That day I'll never forget for as long as I live. He placed a switch blade next to my neck so quickly I could feel the wind whispering across the blade. Turns out, he wasn't a fagot! He told me that he wasn't down, and that he'd cut me up into pieces if I dared look at him. He also promised to tell the whole school about my secret, and he kept his word on his promise.

I was so devastated and depressed my seventh grade year; absolutely everyone including the teachers looked at me differently. I felt like the cavity in someone's mouth, everyone just seemed to want to get rid of me. I had stares that expressed more than I desire to say. I had letters sent to me left and right, and constantly teachers would kick me out of class for disorderly conduct, and I wouldn't even do anything. I asked myself, "How could these people have so much hate toward me? They don't even know me, but they call themselves Christians."

I also said to myself one day, "I'd rather be gay and burn in hell, than to be straight and fake the funk with hateful, life-threatening Christians." Many of my peers preached that God loves the world, but he just doesn't love me.

All I wanted to do was hang out; I wanted my man now more than ever. I needed him to help me feel safe, protected and free.

When I called him, Brian picked up the phone a few times and we talked. I told him about what was happening to me and he shed a few tears for me, but he told me to stay away from him. He told me he had a college career to think about and didn't need the pain and frustration I was going through. So, he'd rather fake it with a girl, than to be who he really was with me. But that was cool though, I could understand now why he did what he did. Back then, of course, I was very upset with him. I even had a P.M.S. moment.

After the conversation with Brian, I told my parents that I wanted to withdraw from the school. They asked me why, and before I knew what I'd done, I had poured myself out to them. I told them everything. All the issues of my heart. They were shocked and confused, but most importantly, they were loving. They knew the demons that were placed on my life because of my uncle, and they prayed to God for my deliverance.

They withdrew me from school, but they also constantly mentioned that I needed to be free. I felt that I was *free* because I got away from all the

s, and I felt like a new year was beginning for
 I entered private school.

Although I didn't initially agree with the
e, I did learn a few things from the Christian
te school they put me in. They said that I
d be safe, but I thought differently because
o-called Christians were predominately the
le who were oppressing me at the other
ɔl.

At that point in my life all I wanted to do
find someone who wasn't afraid to be with
nd hang out. I needed someone who knew
ly what I was going through; I needed a
d.

God Loves You

God loves you is the first and never-en[ding] phrase I heard at Hope Christian Sc[hool]. Every student I met seemed to run u[p to] me and tell me how awesome God is. Even [the] teachers got in on the act. If God was a drug [he] surely had all of them hooked. A simple phra[se,] God loves you—captivated me. Although I [was] feeling like a junkie for the phrase, I really fel[t] I needed someone to love me, at least som[eone] greater than I. But the thought always poppe[d] in my head, how could a big God love me? L[ittle,] poor, gay me? At least, I mean, I was more so [poor] in spirit rather than finances. I seemed to be d[oing] everything wrong and absolutely nothing rig[ht. I] must say, my first thoughts of that private sc[hool] were a great deal different from the thoug[hts I] developed once I started attending.

Whereas I believed that the student[s at] Hope Christian would be the same ole' [gay-]bashing Christians which harassed me at [the] public school, no, these Christians at this sc[hool] actually embraced me. The students and fac[ulty] actually made me feel as though I was apa[rt of] something greater than myself, and to have [that] feeling, well lets just say I'm still ecstatic [and] grateful to them for that.

Right away, I began to see that the school wasn't just filled with a bunch of Christian clowns professing to be all that and a bag of chips, but I saw and felt that the school was bursting with real people with real issues. I saw some individuals who seemed to share hurts that were bigger than mine. Some of my classmates shared with me their past experiences with drugs, loss of family, and everything else in between. Although I didn't feel quite accepted because of my sexual preference, I felt that there was some kind of love going around, the kind of love I didn't get in the public schools. I guess it was the sort of love that only God could give out.

When I entered Hope Christian School everything I knew about God I could write on one side of a three-by-three-inch Post-It. Both of my parents worked on Sundays. The only thing I knew about God was that he was born on Christmas day, and he came back to life on Easter. We usually attended church on those significant holidays. We also managed to bring in each New Year as a family attending church.

In addition to my sporadic church attendance, I often slept through every service I ever attended. Our lack of church attendance perhaps had something to do with why my parents placed me in that Christian private school.

Most of what I knew about Christians when I entered that school was that they hated gays, hated abortion and damned anyone to hell if he blinked wrong.

Nothing about Christian living seemed practical to me, especially when the same people who were casting me down as a sinner going to hell were also fornicating behind the bleachers. I just hated the double standard, and I surely hated the thought process of modern day Christians because they always seemed quick to point the finger, while three fingers were busy pointing back at them. It is very radical and heartless to think that there is a cure for homosexuality, as if it comes and goes with some people. I wish I could have just taken a blue pill and it all be over with. But like many pills, it would have still come with its side effects.

To all the radicals out there who are radical just to be radical and hate gays, there is a place for you. Once a radical, always a radical. Well, I guess that's what they say about gay people, too. Once gay, they will always stray away.

Enough about all the hatred rhetoric. I absolutely hated how harshly I was treated in the public school, but at the Christian private school, I certainly felt much better. The people at Hope Christian School treated me like I was a perfectly normal human. Not like I was a diseased, mangy, stray ally cat. I don't know if it was the teachers, maybe the students or even both, but something about that school made me feel alive, and ultimately restored within me a since of hope. At that time, the school was a predominantly white school. I often considered how the school could of had the perfect combination for discrimination: not only was I black, but I was also gay.

Finishing up my last semester in the seventh grade I felt better about myself. No one knew that I was gay, but everyone knew I wasn't saved by Jesus Christ. I don't know what it was, but I thought it was so amazing that practically everyone in the entire school was praying for me and like three other guys because we had what everyone called *Jesus issues*. At the naive age of thirteen, I didn't understand all the hype in making a vow to a man I didn't see, didn't even know.

The last two times I made a vow to a man, I ended up getting hurt. My uncle forced me to touch him and I vowed my love to Brian, and we were no longer seeing each other. So I asked myself, "What makes this Jesus Christ so special?" He never did anything for me, and most importantly I didn't feel like he set me free from anything. For all I knew, he probably was out to hurt me like the other guys did. Everyone knew my daily excuses. In spite of all my excuses, though, they still prayed for me anyway.

I guess the fact that my fellow classmates prayed for me in spite of my excuses made my seventh grade year one of the best years of my life. I realized that these people, these Christian people, weren't willing to give up on me.

Eighth grade year rolled around, and the teachers were teaching me more than basic math and absolutes. They were teaching basic Bible principles. Aside from their constant teachings in Matthew, Mark, Luke and John, I felt that something big was about to happen in my life. Some say it takes less than ten seconds to rediscover your life, while others say it takes a lifetime. It took me one year, one whole year in the eighth grade to discover who I was.

It's always easy for human beings to put big bad labels on people, especially people they don't know. Why? I guess it's because it gives them a sense of pride about themselves and relieves them of the sins and struggles that haunt them every day. Like a haunted house scares someone when he or she walks through, so is the fear that takes place in this walk called *life*.

There was nothing haunting me more my eighth grade year than my own thoughts of someone discovering my homosexual identity. Not that I was ready to cry or have a fit. It's just that I was not ready to deal with what I went through at my previous school.

I remember walking the halls of that Christian school, always thinking what if they find out? What if someone tells? What if I couldn't make it this time?

I remember strolling down the hallway heading to classroom G22. As I was heading there, I saw an unfamiliar face, but he seemed to know me well. He was dressed in dark blue jeans with a fitted white t-shirt, definitely out of the uniform code. He had a smile which made the butterflies look disgusting and a glow on his face that would put many of the advertised skin cleansers out of business.

The guy called my name and he said, "Hey, I know who you really are, and what you really are."

I stood there for a soft minute, looked at him straight in the eye, and said, "What do you mean?"

He said, " You know what I mean, but don't worry I won't tell."

"Tell what," I said.

"About your alternative lifestyle. Must I go on, Paul?" He told me that he got a word from the Lord that I needed help, and I also needed to change my wicked ways. I was so in awe that this perfect stranger knew so many things about me; he even knew about my uncle. Right then and there I felt that he must have been an Angel of the Lord. His name was Charlie. He told me, as I stood there paralyzed, he mentioned that I needed to be saved by the blood of Jesus Christ and to receive salvation freely.

Still fervently paralyzed or in a trance, the muscles throughout my whole body became intense as my mind began to matriculate this piece of information which seemed to be like a foreign object to my flesh, but a hunger I couldn't quite understand had developed in my inner man. A moment of weakness took place and it shook me, partially scared me, he was offering me something, a gift, that I did not feel I deserved to receive. The words pounced off the tip of his tongue like rain does to a body of water, dipping in and out, each word he said seemed to take on a new meaning, even words I knew so clearly seemed to take a hold of me in a way that I have never felt before then.

He reached his hand out to me once more and told me to quietly repeat after him as I accepted Jesus Christ to be my Lord and Savior.

I felt that if he knew all of this about me, and never knew me personally, then the God that everyone spoke about must have told him something.

I was completely setback by the situation. So much so that I skipped class and ran twelve miles home. I didn't even get tired. I just ran and ran, screaming and shouting the name of Jesus. Screaming and shouting the name of Jesus till I got home. As I finished screaming and shouting with the words Charlie spoke fresh on my mind, I realized that I still had a problem. I still had an unquenchable thirst and lust for men. The thirst. The lust. Never left me. I got saved, but I was not free. Now I had to deal with the blind question of how can I be both gay and Christian at the same time?

If there was anything I learned from one of those teachers, it was that darkness and light can't be in the same room together. So there could be no way possible that I could be both. Naturally, I felt I had to choose a side.

This was my first battle, a spiritual battle for my life. I had to choose to love God with all my heart, soul, and mind or love evil with the same intensity. Needless to say, I chose what I felt comfortable with, and that was darkness. The object of affection for a man grew intensely, and my hormones grew hot and heavy for a man's masculine instruments. That's when I met Dave.

After I met Dave, my life was never the same.

Meet Dave

I vividly remember the night I met Dave. It was a cold winter's night in Miami, cold enough to wear a sweater, but not cold enough to wear a fur coat. So I went with the simple threads of a patriotic looking sweater with fitted blue jeans. One of my male friends dropped me off to the party hosted by some high school kids I didn't know. The air was dry, but still breathable, as I saw the reflection of my breath make strange shapes, as I exhaled with each walk I took to make it to the front door.

I knocked on the door and it swung open. The girl on the other side of the door gestured for me to come in. I had no idea who she was. I'd never met her before. I knew she wasn't the owner of the house, though. I shoved my hands in my pockets, wiped my hard bottom, steal-toe shoes on the dingy welcome mat, and crossed the threshold. I inched my way to one corner of the room. I wasn't trying to be noticed—by anyone. But I, on the other hand, did notice Dave. I spotted him across the room. Among a crowd of about seventy-five people crammed into a spatial cube, he stood out. Something else stuck out, too.

The more I observed Dave, the more I admired his swagger, the more it stuck out. I could feel the blood, hot, boiling, and rushing to the most center point of my body. Luckily, my tight Sean John skinny leg jeans prohibited any bulge that otherwise would have given me away. I tried to remain couture. I stole quick glances of Dave here and there as I constantly changed my position on the wall.

The corner was doing a good job holding me up because I was getting weak in the knees—for Dave. I noticed he wasn't dancing with any of the females, some beautiful, others mediocre in the beauty department. He seemed lifeless, bored with his gorgeous and semi-gorgeous surroundings. They giggled and twirled their hair in their fingers. They flashed every single one of their teeth when they cocked their mouths open, laughing at Dave's jokes. Apparently, he was a very funny character. I noticed I was smiling, inadvertently.

Though I was several feet away from the conversation, I was smiling, too, like one of the females who were lingering on his every word. But I would frown, occasionally, in disgust whenever one of the pretty broads groped Dave's manly muscles. So manly, they protruded through the sleeves of his Polo shirt. My most center point still protruded, too. Finally, Dave stepped away from the air-sucking divas. He needed, no doubt, a breath of fresh air. I seized the opportunity. Before I knew it, my back no longer touched the wall; the corner was not my support. My legs moved, seemingly on their own. They did what my heart told them to do. They found Dave. He was in the far corner of the room, almost in another part of the house. A cool breeze blew from some unknown source.

"Hey, mind if I join you?" I hesitantly asked.

"Naw man, you cool," he responded. His response gave me comfort and I felt more relaxed. I drew nigh to Dave.

"Name's Paul," I reached my hand toward him. My hand itched in anticipation. He looked at it, my hand, as if it was diseased or as if I was speaking sign language. Then, he gripped my hand in acceptance of my introduction. His strong, firm shake soothed my itch.

"Dave."

In further conversation I learned that Dave was a freshman in high school and, well, I was entering the last month of my eighth grade year.

"You're popular with the ladies." I blushed as I stated the obvious.

"Yeah," he kind of sighed, kind of smirked.

"So, why weren't you dancing with anyone? Not your types?"

"Nah. I just don't dance." Dave hung to the wall.

"Oh." It felt a little weird.

Silence.

I hadn't mustered up the nerve to ask him the burning question of the evening. So, I entertained him, as much as I could, with chit chat about other topics: sports, girls, food, school, parents, and winter. The usual guy talk. I needed to know, though, the answer to my question. If I didn't get an answer soon, I might not ever. To me, he looked too good to be gay, and spoke too soft to be straight. I didn't feel like my life was in danger. So why couldn't I ask him this simple question? Did I think he would judge me, ridicule me, expose me? Then...

"Dave, don't take this the wrong way but I thought you were...I mean..." I stuttered. Like vomit, the words just started pouring out, but I was getting chocked on my own vomit. Overwhelming embarrassment forced me to get it out. I didn't want to look like a punk in front of this handsome macho.

"Are you gay?" There it was. I'd asked the taboo question. I slouched in relief, like a burden had been lifted.

Silence fell once again.

He gave me a look that I'd seen before. I didn't know whether to run, duck or hide. What was going on in his mind, I wondered. My eyes frantically searched his face for an inkling of something—rejection, shock, awe, disgust. Something! I couldn't find anything. His glare, first somewhere distant, and then toward me, was bland. Emotionless.

"Yes." He told me very bluntly that he was gay. I was pretty shocked by both his bluntness and above all his sex appeal.

Just my kind of catch. I said in the back of my mind, now I had the opportunity to tell him my secret.

When I told Dave that I shared in the same lifestyle, he brushed me off and told me to leave him alone. He told me that he was still getting over the breakup between him and Leonard. I tried to give him comfort and consultation, but he didn't want to hear me out. His macho persona had melted a little. Though he looked like the Incredible Hulk on the outside, he was more like Phillip Morris on the inside. Noticing that he wanted to be to himself like he told me previously, I just swung him my phone number and left the party. Passing back through the living room to the front door exit, I noticed the swarm of divas had found another victim to shower with their giggles and twirls.

Hoping that he'd give me a call back that night, I decided to walk a few blocks down to the Diner. The stench of dry humping followed me, irritating my nostrils. Scenes of Dave surrounded by high school chaos flickered before me. Like a movie in my head, I replayed our conversation. The shock factor still lingered. Well, to my surprise, he did not call me back that night and I ended up taking a taxi back home an hour before midnight.

Many thoughts crossed my mind. Was Dave really gay? What was his real problem? Would I have an opportunity to see him again?

Dave was beautiful, and in the back of my mind, I was not willing to lose him. So I did what anyone would have done. I caught a taxi back to the house party to see if he was there. To *my surprise*, he was. Dave was all the way in the back keeping to himself, just the way I left him. As I approached him, I was so hoping he wasn't thinking that I was some sort of stalker.

Well what the heck, I said to myself as I continued forward to him anyways. As I continued to walk toward him, he looked toward me. Then with an unexpected gesture, he left from his sobbing post, moved forward two feet and kissed me smack dab on the lips. Of course I was blown away, trying hard to keep my lower instrument in check. The music stopped, the ladies stopped dancing and Dave and I were making out right on the dance floor. I never kissed a guy like that before, but if I had to make a comment I would have to say that *it* was *real good*. Wow! What a night that was.

The passion, the promise, the stimuli, the cravings, all that bundled into one, made me think of the prospect of a new love. Yes, the idea of Dave and I being in love was all that floated across my mind that evening. And right as Dave swept me off my feet, the booming voice of God also caught up with me. How sick and insane it felt to me, to have Dave all over me. His hands, his mouth, his tongue molested me all over again. And I liked it, all over again. Thinking of the commitment I made a few days before, I just knew we had to stop making out on the dance floor.

Cheeks to mouth and mouth to cheeks, it seemed like Dave was slobbering all over me. I felt so weak to the point I was about to collapse. I knew in some way I had to get him to back up, but I wanted more.

Dave seemed to be so aggressive, even more aggressive than my uncle. All I could hear after two minutes of Dave and I smooching was the crowd saying, "Get a room, punks." Right then my senses came back to me, and I knew that I was in trouble. I had already received a label before I even stepped foot in high school. There was no turning back for me now. There are no do-over moments in life. Either you did it or you didn't. I did it.

Finally, Dave felt my uneasiness and he decided to back off of me. Then we both ran out the house and went our separate ways. All I could think about was how much time Dave gave me and the kisses. Oh the kisses. How much sweeter they would have been if we had our own little private space to share. Like I said, Dave was beautiful and I knew a good thing when I saw it. My only caveat was that my conscious kept getting in the way.

The thought and sacrifice for my new found faith was tearing me apart. I felt that since I made the commitment to Jesus Christ, I technically wrote the obituary to my old life. Needless to say, my hormones got in the way, and I could think of nothing more than to be with Dave on a date.

Just a couple of weeks were left for me at the Christian private school and all I could think about was being at the high school with Dave. He and I seemed to connect in ways that I could hardly describe and even care to really understand. All I knew was that I felt good around him and he felt good around me. All the pain from Leonard and Brian left our minds as soon as all the lust and love we had for each other began.

With a few weeks left in middle school, all the eighth graders were preparing for the pass-the-torch dance. They didn't just call it the eighth grade prom like the other schools in the area did. With good reason, though, because it was nothing like the average eighth grade prom. This ceremony was highly charged with scriptures, pastoral visits and parents. Each student was allowed to invite one saved friend, and two parents. All I could think about was Dave, but I knew if he showed up to the pass-the-torch dance, it would be heavy suspect. It surely wouldn't look right, and I had no idea if he was saved or not. I felt like I was lost in the shuffle of the unknown, waiting to be recognized and discovered by Jesus.

I ended up bringing my parents with me and never told Dave about the event. The one thing that made Dave so special to me was that he listened to me for whom I was and personally understood what I went through. As a boy, he was raped by his cousin, and he told me that homosexuality was just the norm for him. He said from the time he was two, his thirteen year old cousin used to show himself to him, wanting him to pet him.

I was so surprised how easy Dave was willing to share his life and passions with me. Every day I saw him, I saw such a bright side to him; he just got cuter and cuter to me.

The end of the eighth grade and the end of middle school was coming up for me. My parents deeply encouraged me to continue private school, but I rebelled and told them no. So I got what I wanted and ended up at Blackwell High School with Dave.

High Times

Times were good for me as I began my freshman year at Blackwell High School. The smell of new desk, lemon scented classrooms and new people of all shapes, sizes and colors gave me a level of excitement for school that I could not ignore. Even the plain white paint on the walls gave me new meaning to school, and oh the courtyard was so huge; the many flowers cheered us on as the magnolia seemed to dance with the wind and the sunflowers smiled across the lawn. The artificial waterfall was a sanctuary for birds to come and rest while pecking at the cool water.

The teachers were pretty cool too, they weren't quick to judge, and although I missed that one-on-one time I received at Hope Christian School. At Blackwell High School, no one seemed to talk about Jesus, instead, they mostly talked about the hottest trends in music and fashion, and of course the topic of sex was not a luxury there, it was a school wide staple.

Everyone seemed to get along in their particular groups, the Geeks, Goths, Jocks and the Gays. Most of all, though, I liked the fact that I got the man that I was hoping for and my grades were even good. You couldn't have asked for a more pleasant time.

My exposure to illegal green herbs, or better known as weed and a variety of weed combinations had me wide open. Yes, I was smoking weed and feeling good about it.

I was introduced to *Black&Milds* in the seventh grade by a classmate of mine, this was right around the time Brian had left me and I felt so lonely and depressed. I loved the sweet smell of *Black&Milds*, the aroma often placed me in a trance as the pressures of life seemed to whisk away. In the back of my mind I felt that it was perfectly legal for a seventh grader to smoke *Black&Milds* since they sell them at every corner store I knew at the time, and the clerk surely didn't care to ask me for identification.

Upon entering Blackwell High School *Black & Milds* just didn't do the trick. My adventures with weed gave me a for-sure feeling of being a man! Well, at least partially. It's strange. It's like I know I have the tools...the tools men have that bring pleasure to women, but my body desires another use for them, at least a use that is far unnatural from what God intended them to be used for.

After school would finish, Dave and I would roll up a quick one. Of course we made sure the windows were up tight in his car, and we just smoked out in the school parking lot like we were the coolest dudes in school. We turned the

AC on its highest level and the music even higher as we just got high as a kite making straight and gay jokes, we also filled each other in on the latest gossip, we had competitions to see who could stutter the longest and we even had red eye competitions. In case you didn't know what red eye competitions were, we basically smoked so much weed and paid for the other person's dime bag for the next time we smoked if his eyes were the reddest. We had an extensive collection of weed and cologne in the car. Sean John Cologne wasn't around back then, so we settled for Tommy, Fahrenheit and a few others. Dave made my life so much better, and those times he and I spent alone in the car smoking out were priceless.

I think my mom knew I smoked. One day after school, after Dave and I rolled a blunt, and turned his Impala into a hotbox, I went home. On the drive to my house, we rode with the windows rolled all the way down, trying to air out the stench of burning illegal green herbs. I bathed my body and clothes in cologne. The goal was to not smell like I'd just finished getting high and to not get caught. I opened the car door, ran to my front door, and ran to my room, leaving a lingering aroma of cologne along my path.

"Hey mom. Bye mom. I'll be right back." I moved fast, barely planting a kiss on her cheek.

Once in my room, I peeled of the cologne-soaked clothes and tossed them in my dirty hamper, where the different fragrances collided, forming a singular scent altogether. Changing into my comfy pajamas, I flopped onto the bed. It was messy. Needed to be changed. I didn't care. I dozed off.

"Why do you drench your clothes in cologne, Paul, knowing they will be washed?" My mother's question disturbed my slumber.

"Huh?" I moaned.

"Paul? Do you hear me talking to you?"

"Yeah, Ma. Yeah. I hear you."

"What a waste," I heard her mummer. She piffled through my dirty clothes, smelling each garment. Whatever she was searching for, whatever she found, she never harassed me about it. Although she knew something was up, as long as my grades were right, she just didn't trip about it.

Outside of smoking my brain to oblivion, I loved the frequent dates to the movies, nail salon and spa. I saw Dave as like my other half. I would have never thought to let him go. He never really forced himself onto me except that one night we first met at the house party. Dave was so cute in all his ways; he knew how to make me comfortable. When I was sad, he would read me a poem from one of his favorite poets. When I was cold he often cuddled me till I was his temperature, when I was hungry he took the time to grill me a meal and he even was generous when it came down to money, not that I needed it.

With the high times of high school, I learned even more about myself. I learned that the independent God given spirit which God had given to me was more by choice and not of something I was necessarily born with. I'm not saying that everything was peaches and cream my freshman year in high school because, of course, I was being ridiculed by all the gay comments and invisible tomatoes being thrown at my face. What those straight people didn't understand about me was the more they barked, the more I relished my *gay pride*. Who would want to be around folks who ran around throwing up hateful signs like participants of the *Tea Party*?

I hate to compare being gay to the civil rights movement, but I must say, that fight which I continuously fought was like that of the civil rights era. I was a fifteen year old fighting for freedom, justice, and the American way. The only problem with being a part of a fight is finding the right people to fight with.

Outsiders' general idea of gay men is that we are weak, cry babies, hiders and runners. Although that general idea may have applied to most of the high school punks, there were quite a few who would stand up and beat up football players. Those were the ones I found *very* attractive, and the urge to cheat on Dave always crossed my mind.

Although Dave never hinted at it, I was always insecure at the thought of his turning straight. He was so cute, that I just knew the girls would ambush him the very moment he made such an announcement. But to my amazement, he didn't. He stayed loyal to me, and that's what made him to be all the more special to me.

As I was saying about that civil rights stuff, being gay in the ninth grade was more than an internal battle from the bullies. Most of the jocks who thought they were big time loved to judge me, the cheerleaders loved me, and the parents looked down at me. This, of course, was something I witnessed before, but all I wanted was for this constant torment and finger pointing to end. Individuals with alternative lifestyles deserve the same opportunities and equality as those who are heterosexual. That's all I really was asking for. Equality.

I so appreciated having Dave because he always seemed to have the right words to say to me, and he definitely knew how to make me laugh. He was such a sweet heart. I remember when I was having a bad day once; Dave pulled me to the side and sung lullabies in the court yard for everyone to hear while embarrassing himself. I was so crammed with laughter that I forgot all the problems I was having that day.

So how did I end my freshman year of high school? Well, I started the *gay club*, and it was a great opportunity for us gays to voice our opinions about how we felt about different issues on campus. Some of the issues ranged from the simple name calling to the very serious 'bullying'. That year we had about ten members. Six of the members had slept with Dave the previous year.

In my opinion, those guys who Dave slept with looked a little too gay to me, but that's just my opinion. Although Dave and I did have sexual relations, we never went all the way. I was always afraid of where all the way would take me. As much as my hormones were clouding my mind and stimulating certain parts of my body, I dared not talk about it. Going all the way was still uncomfortable for me.

Lucky for me, Dave was understanding. He never pushed or manipulated me into feeling like I needed to go all the way with him. He never insinuated his leaving me for another guy, another lover, who would go all the way. Instead, Dave showered me with flowers, chocolates and extravagant gifts. He had no problem buying me fourteen karat gold and he charmed me when he bought me this cool Motorola Phone. Dave was the best friend I ever had. Those were the good ole' days, Dave and I sharing moments, memories, and motivation to keep each other together. I really, really can't stop talking about Dave; he was my hero, my lover, and my best friend.

Just as quickly as the ninth grade came and went, so did the tenth and eleventh grades. My eleventh grade year was truly my highest time in high school, and I'm happy to be able to tell you about it.

As my junior year rolled around, I realized that I was going to lose the one love that stood by me in the midst of my differences. And of course that one love was Dave, who was then a senior. Thinking about the thought of losing Dave was like thinking about the thought of losing the sun; we know when that happens pretty much everything dies. A lot began to die in me, as Dave continually eluded me about going away to college. All I ever talked about was how to keep him in Miami with me. I didn't want to lose my best friend and *lover*. I felt that Dave completed me; he gave me attention like no one else could. He seemed to be the only man who could truly fulfill my needs.

So as it was, my highest time in high school was my junior year. This year was the year that Dave and I totally made a splash at the prom.

Besides college, all that was on Dave's mind was the prom. Now, one thing I might not have mentioned about Dave is that he was an excellent dancer. I was just as surprised to learn about this hidden attribute, too, especially considering the fact that he wasn't dancing at all the night of our first kiss. I, on the other hand, could barely do a two-step. I never met such an all-around guy as Dave. It's as if I had won the lottery with Dave.

Sometimes love could be just that, like winning the lottery. In the pursuit of happiness, I realized that I often came short of a few tickets, but when Dave and I found each other... Well, you know the rest. I hit the jack pot.

So, it was time for Dave to choose what he was going to wear. I mean there were so many rude comments coming from the other students, like who's going to wear the dress? Other comments were made, such as there can't be two prom queens. Some students even had the nerve to make such provocative comments as, "wash your booty before you get fruity."

I was hurt. Yes, I was hurt beyond measure, but I was determined not to let what everyone else said about me or Dave take our moment away. Dave with his usual nonchalant self, didn't even let one word they said get to him. I just could not see how he had the strength to withstand such evil.

As the senior prom was less than three weeks away, I was contemplating whether I should go all the way and give up the goods, or wait for another moment. I know that this may sound strange, but although I was gay, I still felt pretty uncomfortable about the issue. I balked at the thought of sex, and hated the allurement to other things which I will not mention.

I know that I wanted to do something special for Dave because it seemed to me to be one of the last times that we'd see each other. He had already made his big plans to travel up to Kentucky for college, and I felt stuck in the middle of a maze of letting go and holding back.

After the Prom

Dave and I had such a good time together. We could have easily fooled anyone to believe that we were lifetime partners. A great deal of people surprisingly accepted us for the lifestyle we chose, and I even had a chance to dance with a few girls. Instantly, the dance with the first girl brought back memories of when Sandra and I danced at the fifth grade prom. As I danced with that first girl, I couldn't help myself again, that tiny urge in my body forced me to feel a little uncomfortable in the tux.

I'm not sure if the girl noticed or not, but I knew that something once more was going on in my body at the mere thought of dancing with—being with--women that I could not explain. Realizing that I spent close to ten minutes with the first girl, I walked back over to dance with the dashingly cute Dave, who had on a fitted black striped tux with a blue vest; of course he and I were twins.

Dave was a hit, he was smashingly beautiful, and he danced with such a silent frequency. You would have thought he was dancing with the wind. I had so much fun. After the prom, Dave and I made sure to take pictures, and we officially declared a friendship forever, no matter what happened.

We exited the hotel lobby and together in the corner, kissing and hugging, kissing and hugging as we watched the cars stroll by while constantly singing romantic blues to each other.

"I got you babe," we hummed.

"They say we're young and we don't know. We won't find out until we grow," I sang in Dave's ear.

"Well I don't know if all that's true, 'cause you got me and I got you..." he responded, "Babe," and kissed my forehead. I melted in his grasp.

"I got you to hold my hand," he squeezed my hand like a deacon giving a new member the right hand shake of fellowship.

"I got you to understand."

"I got you to walk with me."

"I got you to talk with me."

"I got you to kiss goodnight," and he leaned in for a smooch. That was it. I was gone. Under. Drowning in the emotions that erupted from our lips. I surely loved those tender lips. People ask me today who is a better kisser, male or female. Personally, I think that females are better kissers because they get very, very passionate with their kisses. Whereas a guy for the most part loves to stay at stage one. Women love to go to stage three and four, all the way down the throat. I know that all men, hu-men, were created equal--not when it boils down to kissing. The woman reigns supreme.

    Dave and I were kissing still. In my head, I finished singing the lyrics to the song: I got you to hold me tight. I got you, I won't let go. I got you to love me so. I got you, babe. I got you, babe. I got you, Dave. I got you, Dave.

    "I got you, too," he chimed. Did he hear me? Was I singing aloud? I could have sworn I was singing only in my head. I finally came to the conclusion that Dave and I had a special connection, a telepathic connection. He knew the most inner me, and I him. We could hear each other's thoughts.

    Dave had rented us a hotel room for the night; we sat there in the corner of the bench waiting on the taxi for an hour to take us twenty minutes across town. When we finally arrived to the hotel at about one thirty in the morning, we were too tired to do anything. So we just decided to take off all the makeup, cosmetics, prom clothes and go to sleep.

    That's when I felt something. Apparently Dave did not want to go to sleep because he obviously had an erection. Not knowing what to do at this point, I pretended to close my eyes and played sleep. Well, he grabbed a hold of my undergarments, and that's when I ran. I tossed the covers aside in a heartbeat and dashed into the bathroom. He yelled out, "What's wrong?" I lied and told him nothing was wrong. I knew what he wanted. I just couldn't make my mind to take it to that other level with Dave. I just could not do what he wanted me to do. Dave was hurt, he was devastated, he was cussing, because the whole time I was dating him, I never could give up the goods like that. Something deep inside of me wouldn't let me.

Tap, tap, tap. It was Dave, knocking on the bathroom door. While he stood on one side, I sat with my back against the other.

"Are you seeing someone else," Dave asked, nonchalantly. I smiled just a little; half frowned because I could still hear the anger, frustration in Dave's voice.

"No. Of course not," I said. That was the truth. I heard Dave release a heavy sigh. It was a sigh of frustration and relief. He was just angry with me, and rightfully so. So, I just stayed to myself in the bathroom till he cooled down. Dave was definitely a very handsome young man. I just couldn't reconcile myself to having him or another guy sodomize me. I personally thought that it was nasty and all out disgusting, but I also knew that as a rule of thumb to being a homosexual, I would have to give up the goods to fit in. Many men, including Dave, were telling me how good it felt, and that I didn't know what I was missing.

The hard part, or should I say the easy part, was that I knew there was nothing but turds and farts being released from that section. And based upon the last time I did a number two, it didn't feel or smell real good down there. That moment after the prom was the moment when I really began to start questioning myself. Questioning who I really was, and questioning the relevant fact of what was I really doing in that hotel room with Dave, knowing that I wasn't ready to give it up? I wasn't ready to bend over and show the world that I, too, can be in the position of a dog.

Standing to my feet, I finally released the knob of that bathroom door and stepped once more into the room, I saw a naked and fully erect Dave signaling for me to come to him. I did come to him, and looking at his handsome physique and well sculptured frame got me hypnotized for a moment. Then, we started passionately kissing. He began to rub on my shoulders, stomach and everywhere in between. I was taken, taken by the outpouring of his spirit.

I was taken by the dreaminess of his flesh. My mind was in more than fantasy land. This was the real thing happening. Our energies surged the air. As he lay my body across the bed face down, guilt came once more to me. I tried to ignore it. I could feel the heat seeping through his flesh as he moved closer toward me. Operation penetration was in affect. He touched my waist with his hand, gently, and spoke something to me. I couldn't hear him; I couldn't make out what he said because right at that juncture I felt as if a still small voice said, **"Paul, what am I to you?"** And all I could think of was what did that mean. Without hesitation, I jumped to my hands and knees. My feet scurried to find solid ground. Standing across from Dave on the opposite side of the bed, I asked Dave that same question. He was speechless and clueless. Not a word drizzled out of his mouth. I could tell his whole frame of thought had changed as well. His entire body went limp.

    I, too, was confused, but it took me two years later to realize that those words were my saving grace. They saved me from the passions and ultimately from abomination. Perhaps while reading this story you have already cast your stereotypes on me, passed your judgment, and that's cool. But I want you to know that I'm trying to keep this story as real as possible. These are the things I've gone through; this is my life. Moments I'm not necessarily proud of, but hey, what can I say?

    Something else happened that night after the prom. Dave and I broke up. We both felt that it was the best thing for the both of us. I wasn't too saddened by the whole thing, but I can tell he was. This was the dude who introduced me to weed smoking, double kissing, and told me to be proud of my sexuality. He was the man who I always dreamed about, but afterwards the only place that I could see him, was in my dreams.

    Dave was the type of guy who was very, very unpredictable. Of course he made me laugh, made me cry, but most importantly, he made me feel loved. I felt like he was the extension of a relationship I was always longing for, but too embarrassed to talk about in front of my parents. My parents knew that I was in an intimate relationship with Dave, but they tried to deny it. My brothers and sisters also rejected me, and Dave seemed to be one of the few who loved me for me.

Many people say, "How does the role change when a man loves another man. How does the affection for that partner manifest itself into something beautiful and magnificent?" I personally don't know the answer to that. But I do know that love has no boundaries; it transcends past race, gender, and even sexual preference.

My love for this man taught me that my love for the man Christ Jesus had to start to take root and blossom somewhere, somehow. And that somewhere, somehow began my senior year.

Senior Year

Some would have thought that the nickname for our school was party; it just was the honest fact that we had some sort of party like every day. Chicken strips party on Monday. We had a secretary party on Tuesday, the Principal's honor roll party on Wednesday, and basketball team party on Thursday. There was a football party on Friday. Over and over again, parties, pizza, chicken and hamburgers were the life of my senior year, not to mention the cakes. Everybody seemed to have a good time their senior year. Of course I wasn't. I was missing Dave, and there wasn't the slightest thing I could do about it.

I began to have very vivid fantasies about Dave, thinking about him standing naked in the hotel room, hoping he said come here again. Wishing he could just breathe on me for a second and I'd be alright. But no, there was no more Dave, all there was, was me.

I was terribly surprised how the seniors didn't pick on me as much as I was picked on my previous years. It actually felt a little depressing that no one was noticing me. Maybe it was because I took off the high heels, high water jeans, and erased the makeup off my face. My senior year was the first year of high school that I had a reasonable amount of normalcy in my appearance, or whatever one would call normal looking for a guy. I pretty much outgrew the so-called gay look, and besides, those high heels caused at least six twisted ankles and a fractured back. Guys are just not meant to wear high heels. I, on the other hand, strutted in them heels like a pro. I would kill a run way while being fashionably gorgeous.

Reminiscing on Dave was what I did best my senior year. Sometimes that boy drove me crazy. Sometimes the very thought of him had me sizzling in my seat. At the time of my senior year, I didn't know why this little life of mine was changing, but it wasn't by my will; it had to be a little bit of something else.

Running into the guy's locker room to get a sneak peek of the football players was never the same anymore; it was different, very different. Dave and I suffered many bloody noses and bumps on our heads because of it, but it was exciting. It not only stimulated our hearts but also something else. It was always fun to watch the big football players get all the girls, all the groupies. I just counted the ten and knew that each girl that slept with the player thought that she had a promise for her future, a future money maker. My dreams about the players were a little different, and that dream was based on pure lust and entertainment. I couldn't help but think about it, but Dave, oh Dave would pull me into him when he saw that I was looking at the players too hard.

So basically my senior year sucked. No Dave. No kids running around picking at me, and for once in a while I had no man in my life. One thing that always seemed to torment my soul that year was, why oh why did my uncle abuse me? Maybe then, just maybe I would be living a different life. I realized the drive that was still there for women while at the prom the previous year. But I just could not figure out how I would be able to change. What would make me different? Up to this point in my life, the only person who I had sex with was Sandra Lopez, and that was way back in middle school. Yes, I've dated other guys and we've done things, but not to the level of Sandra and I.

I, Paul Stringer, was so confused my senior year, until I felt like I wanted to puke each day I went to class. What was so wrong about being gay? This one question constantly streamed through my head. What was so right about being straight? Another question beamed through my head: Why can't I just be both? A lot of things just weren't making since in my life at that point. A lot of confusion, a lot of corrupt thoughts, pretty much a lot of mess.

Even surfing through the net seemed harder my senior year. Usually I'd just go to the gay porn sites, but the allure of the so-called straight sites also took up my attention. I don't know; I just didn't know what was going on with me. The thought of me losing my mind could have been an explanation to all problems I was going through. I honestly felt like a woman going through her menstrual cycle. With each month, I knew that the pain of life was coming, and believe me, I had some mood swings.

    The one good thing that came out of my senior year was a decent conversation with my younger siblings. They actually spoke to me as if I were *human*, not some stray dog that shouldn't have been born! They just talked to me about some of the peer pressures they were going through. They asked for advice on certain issues, especially the issue of sex. And the most compelling thing of all, my brother who was born after me, gave me a hug for the first time.

    I explained to him my dilemma, and that my affections for guys was not for every guy. I shared with him and my other sibling my battles, my weaknesses and my past lovers. During one conversation in particular, my siblings and I all broke out in tears, because for the first time I explained to them who I was and why. Of course they knew about the incident with my uncle, but they still didn't know the force that such an incident had on my life. I guess they thought that I could just shake it off and pretend that it never happened.

    How can anyone shake off such a series of events? No counselor, doctor, or whoever could make me forget what I had to do to make my uncle happy.

Senior prom? I didn't go to the senior prom. I did not envision myself going to the prom solo; besides, I think it would have brought back memories of Dave and me. You know how they say a good man is hard to find? Well, he was that good man. And he was nowhere to be found.

It was the end of my secondary education, my high school escapade, my senior year. I walked across the stage, diploma in my right hand and a peace of mind in the other. My parents were so proud of me. I was their first child to graduate. As a matter of fact, I was their first in just about everything except giving them grandkids, but we'll talk about that later.

So, my senior year was over with and now was the time to take on a new life and a new responsibility. The college life was calling me and boy was I ready.

Look Both Ways before You Cross

How can a man be a man if he does not know why he is a man? How could a man engage himself in life without being given the willingness and opportunity to explore what's out there? Better yet, what makes a man a man? I have had many people come up to me and judge me, saying, "Oh, you ain't no man, because you gay. You just another one of them booty chasers." Or, they may hurl my way the famously played-out slur, "You ain't nothing but a punk!"

Many times I wanted to say to those fools, "Hey guy, I'm packing more heat in my pants than your lady could handle." But is that what makes me a man? The size of the anatomy snuggled between my legs? Or let me guess, because I can diss another guy and get my voice louder than his, this made me a man. If that's what it takes to be a man, then being a man definitely wasn't for me. I'm about treating people with love and honest respect, no matter their situation.

I remember the times in elementary school when the crossing guard used to say look both ways before you cross. Well, that's the exact science of my thinking when I first began college. I decided to look both ways, and both ways were to experiment with both guys and girls. I pretty much came up with my own conclusion, which was in order to better like guys, I must first like girls and vice versa. I know that this sounds crazy, but it was my frame of thought at the time. Yes, I know that it was stupid, petty and dumb, but hey I was a fresh college kid, straight out of a frustrating year of high school. So, upon entering Francis State University in Tallahassee, Florida, I began practicing bisexualism.

I would have flings with the girls in the morning and sneak out with guys at night. Thinking nothing wrong with it at the time, I felt no difference in enjoyment with one or the other, with the exception that girls almost always wanted to have that emotional attachment. I wasn't really down for that emotional attachment stuff.

Looking both ways, for the most part, was fun for me. There were no strings attached like that of a relationship. And the best part of it all was that I was getting the best of both worlds, or so I thought.

The lust from my heart was overshadowing my mind, and therefore everything I was doing, I felt right about it. The deep pleasure and satisfaction of a sexual urge fulfilled was what I loved and desired for each and every day. Yet, I was burning; I was burning my relationship with God and my relationship with myself. Many days of my collegiate freshman year, I didn't know who

I wanted to be. All in all, I realized that I just wanted to be accepted at all costs.

I was clearly trying to find my identity, my strength, and most importantly my preference. As I looked both ways, I could clearly see that both sides had its positives and negatives. Therefore, I came up with the conclusion that I am supposed to be with a woman, but the drive to be with a man also spoke volumes to me.

Let me break it down a little further. A woman is good; she's the bearer of fertility. Without a woman I wouldn't even be here today. A woman has extraordinary powers because she is able to know things that many times we men try to keep secret.

Now as far as my wanting a man, he's the thing I'm attracted to because he knows what it takes to be me. He usually has more physique than a woman, and he doesn't fuss, wine and complain like a woman does. Also, if it wasn't for a man, I wouldn't be here today. So here's the conflict: How am I to make a sound choice on whether to be with a man or a woman when both are the reason that I'm here today.

That's why looking both ways before crossing into one sex is not a bad idea. At least I thought it was.

Pimps, whores and gangbangers all know about the steady trap in their lives. Whether it be a gun placed in someone's face, a prostitute getting trains run on her for petty cash, or just an ordinary son-of-a-gun taking advantage of the brokenhearted and becoming the C.E.O. of a large organization of prostitutes. However it's sliced or diced, there's a game to be played, and whether it is seen or unseen, someone usually ends up on the losing side of things. That somebody is usually the weakest link. Although pimps, whores and gangbangers are nothing positive to talk about, looking both ways like I did can sometimes make them look like a saint.

From what I've read from the good book, *the Bible* that is, a homosexual is pretty much a male cult prostitute. Wow! Did I see myself as a male cult prostitute? Of course not. But it's hard to admit, it gets confusing at times.

My father used to tell me all the time, don't let your hormones control you. You control them. And that was exactly my problem when I entered college. I didn't have control of my hormones; they were set on fire for pleasure, and it all seemed to make sense as I looked both ways.

The rush to have sex again and again without any consequences was nearly uncontrollable. Except for the thought of contracting STDs, nothing or no one was unattainable. I felt practically unstoppable. STDs. They, alone, were my kryptonite. They were about the only thing that kept me in check between what I was going to do, and when I was going to do it.

I can admit it now; I was sick of the way I was living and still a little sick today. But I was sick because I was living such a high-risk life.

Who would imagine the value I was losing, the soul that was burning, and the people I was abusing. Some call it night walker; I call it hood stalker. Every day I felt like I was continuing the same rotation because I knew every time this girl had her period, and every time my boyfriend was ready. Correction, he was always ready. It was the girlfriend who always seemed to be the problem. I can recall many times I tried to be romantic, and some of the women I was messing with just brushed me off like an unwanted cockroach. The thing that upset me the most about my whole freshman situation was the general fact that neither the guy nor the girl knew I was looking both ways. It just seemed to be too obvious for me not to get caught. But then again, I was good at being incognito.

Life becomes very complicated when you do things outside of the normal order and principal of what God has in store for you. When we do things outside of the will of God, that's when things get messy. And things couldn't have gotten any messier until I found out about the conception of my son.

You never really know the true meaning of life, till you are on the verge of giving birth to a new life. I thought that I used protection every time my girlfriend and I became one, but I guess I messed up somewhere along the way. All of that doesn't matter now; I could only recall the chill that I felt when she announced to me over the phone that she was late. Nonchalantly I brushed her off because I had no Earthly idea what she was talking about; we didn't have any events planned for that evening. Then she paused for a brief two seconds and with a higher clearer pitch she said that she was late on her period and did a pregnancy test.

    I nearly tested out a big oak tree in the median because I almost lost control of my vehicle with the news of her pregnancy. I changed all plans of spending time with my boyfriend and shot right over to my girlfriends place to see the validity in her comment. Sure enough the test came up positive and my son was scheduled to be deployed from his mother's womb nine months later.

    When my girlfriend was three months pregnant, I was still switching lanes. Of course at three months we didn't know what sex the child was going to be, but four months after the three, I found out it was going to be a boy, tears began to erupt from my eyes. It was as if heaven decided to open up the pores in me and let me rain and rain tears all over the floor of the hospital. It was a crazy moment for me, as I stared looking at my girlfriend, watching as the OBGYN showed us the baby kicking in her womb.

Kicking and moving, my baby boy was preparing to be delivered.

Deliverance

The thought of the arrival of my son had me thinking about a lot of things. Who am I? What am I? What am I to do? This was also the summer leading up to my sophomore year in college. I decided to take the summer session off to help my girlfriend through the pregnancy and help her out with the baby. He was expected to officially arrive on earth in August.

While we were waiting on my son-to-be's debut, I was taking my girlfriend back and forth to the doctor's office, I was trying to figure out how to tell her about the double life I was leading. I mean honest to God, I was not expecting to have a child my freshman year in college. As a matter of fact, the thought of having children was not even in my book of things to do before I die. Knowing what I've gone through in my childhood made me fear having children, especially a son..

Many say that the truth hurts and I know it does, but getting the truth out to my baby mama Kim at the same time she was in pain and agony with baring my son would hurt even more than the labor pains, I concluded. So I decided to not break the news until after the baby was born. In the meantime, I decided to cut off the guy I was seeing. I just wanted to focus in on my girl and this new life that was ready to begin.

In my mind, I kept mulling over how to break the news of my bisexual habits to Kim. I was also thinking a lot about my son. Thinking about how I was going to protect him, keep him away from uncles. I also wondered if he would be born like me, with homosexual tendencies, or would he have his rightful chance at being normal like everyone else? Would he have the sincere chance to be free to choose what he wanted to be? I guess that fatherly potion was kicking me in the head because all I wanted to do was protect my unborn son from the outside world. I wanted to do what his mom did for him in the womb for nine months. Nourish him. Guard him. Protect him. Love him.

Frustrated, excited and still addicted to thoughts of wrestling with naked men under sheets, on sofas, in narrow hallways...stop. I had to murder these thoughts. But how? I decided to seek wisdom in a place I did not see for years. I went to church.

"Dear heavenly Father, we thank you for your sweet commune. We thank you, Father, for your fresh anointing. We thank you, Father, for the lives that are here--Father God. We thank you for your son Jesus, who died and rose again one day for the deliverance of our sins."

As soon as I heard Pastor Willie Brown mention the name of Jesus at *Faith at First Church*, I stood up and realized I'd heard that name before. I was not familiar with all that other mess he had spoken, but I did know the name of Jesus. My abrupt leap from my seat caught the attention of many parishioners, and the pastor. He said to me, "Come on son, come on up, the Lord is waiting for you. Salvation is yours, saith the Lord, and it's time for you to be set free." He'd noticed me, picked me out of the crowd. He spoke directly to my situation. It felt like something was about to erupt inside me.

"Hallelujah!" I shouted. "Hallelujah!" Like vomit, the words spewed from my lips. My lungs felt like they were about to explode. They hurt. I was just screaming, wailing and screaming in the church. The more I screamed, the more I spewed hallelujah praises, the more my lungs hurt.

I started making my way to the alter. The falling tears from my persistent wailing blurred my vision. I could barely see past my nose, but comforting hands from members of the congregation guided me to where I stood, smack dab in the middle of the alter, collapsed at waist, squeezing my torso—the pain in my lungs intensified. The pastor directed me once more to salvation, and he professed deliverance over my life. He took some cooking oil and smeared it over my forehead. He said all kinds of stuff, things I don't remember. But the two most uplifting things he said to me was to receive deliverance in the name of Jesus, and he prophesied that my son's name would be called Eliphalet. His prophesy sort of freaked me out because I didn't tell him about a son. Better yet, what else did he know about me? I wondered.

I was afraid because I knew that this preacher man was a true man of God, and if God allowed him to see my sins, I knew that I would be put to shame. He told me one last thing before I went back to my seat. He said, "Son, treat that woman right. Buy her the best flowers you can find and seal it with an olive branch. Be prepared for tough times and tough decisions."

I said, "Yes sir," and walked back to my seat.

By the time I got two rows away from my seat, the tears that had only moments ago stopped abruptly began to pour, and the light from the chandelier began to shine over me. I felt like a new man, a man of integrity, a man of strength, a man who would not back down into the traps any longer. I felt deliverance.

"Push, push," the doctors repeated. "Push, push," they coached my girlfriend for an hour as she prepared to give way for a new life. All the while, the head of my son Eliphalet was sliding from between my girlfriend's legs. Just as much as I received deliverance on that particular Sunday, my son was also delivered on a Sunday. Finally, I thought, he gets a chance to see what the world is really made of; finally he gets to be the man that I've been struggling to be. But there was something wrong; there was something unnaturally wrong with little baby Eliphalet. Something the doctor didn't notice when Eliphalet was in the womb, but we found out that he was born with two organs. He had both the showing of a small vaginal opening and the packaged sexual reproduction organs of a male.

The doctor spoke to us both and kind of told us what to do. He said it was best to do nothing because Eliphalet was too young. So that's what we did, *nothing*. We followed the doctor's advice to wait till he got older. I was furious; I was so upset with myself. I was upset with God and my family. I was just so upset that Eliphalet was to grow up and go to school being different like me. I really started to blame myself. I figured the only logical reason for his being born that way was because I was swinging both ways. I was broken—heartbroken.

So I told her.

It was during an evening of bliss that I decided to spill the beans; we were having a good time at this Authentic Mexican Restaurant. The live Mexican band which played that evening did an amazing job, they looked like the three musketeers except they were armed with a drum, violin and a trumpet. Kim loves to dance, so we took to the dance floor, doing the Rumba,

Macarena and the twist. We held each other tight as we swung around and around like little kids, barely making a scratch on the floor. After we danced I ordered Gordita De Nata for dessert, it's a type of Mexican pastry which both her and I just loved. Baby Eliphalet was being watched by a trusted friend of ours, all I could think of was him while at the restaurant.

    The waiter carefully brought out the dessert as Kim's deep brown eyes grew wider, and her baby face dimples spread across her cheeks. She was a very beautiful African-American woman, that night she was dressed in a sexy red dress which fit her curves appropriately and her stilettos drew eyes from the guys far and near. She could pass for Indian with her naturally long and luscious black hair, just like Pocahontas. I kept fighting back and forth in my mind, *how was I going to tell this beautiful woman my secret lifestyle I've been living for years.*

    I waited for her to finish dessert and for the band to simmer down the volume a bit, and then, right then is when I released my soul to her. I told my girlfriend Kim all that I was doing, all that my bisexual relationships entailed.

    She was awe struck. Waived me off like a liar and looked for the waiter to ask for the bill. I repeated myself once more, she still didn't budge, still didn't want to believe the truth which I was dishing her. This was not a reality T.V. show, but the tightening of my heart and pressures in my chest felt like I was on T.V., it felt like a director just snatched everything I had from under me and told me to do the part again. When Kim heard the silence between her and I, right then she knew that I was serious. She saw the verdict of guilty written all across my face, and then, right then in this fine Authentic Mexican Restaurant is when Kim did the unthinkable.

She Screamed….

She was hurt beyond measure and pushed me away. She said she didn't know who I was and blamed my heathen ways on the reason our son was born with both male and female instruments. I was twenty-one years and I didn't know what to say to her, how to respond to her pain. More or less, I didn't really know what to do I needed time to think, to deeply ponder. So I left the restaurant and hitched a ride to the nearest saloon, Y'Resim. I thought it was a funny name for a bar, but the taxi cab driver said it served great beer, over 101 kinds. When I stepped out the taxi, onto the sidewalk, and into the bar I felt heaviness. It wasn't my heaviness alone. It seemed to be the ambiance. The look of gloom painted the faces of the patrons as I trudged through the thick, thick atmosphere. I sat on a stool, swiveled around, and ordered a rum and coke from the bar tender.

"Cash or tab?" he asked.

"Let's run a tab," I replied.

"Happy to serve the heavy laden," he grinned, and crafted my beverage with more rum than coke.

At first, I thought about nothing. I stared mindlessly into space. Around or about my third or fourth drink, my inner voice boomed as I listened to my thoughts. It was as if I was speaking on a megaphone to myself. She didn't want to be bothered with me, I thought. But I could understand why. I just couldn't take the stress, yelling, and blaming me for everything any longer at that hospital. I downed the corner of whisky that I swirled around in my glass.

"Let me get another one of these," I slammed the glass down on the counter top.

I told the bartender to keep pouring, keep giving me cup after cup. All the while I was spilling my guts to him about my son, and my past sexual relations. I don't think he really cared what I said, as long as those tips were going in his tipping jar. All I could recall him saying was yep, yes and I understand. I could have easily mistaken him for a Parrot.

After placing myself one hundred dollars in the hole on liquor, I decided to call a taxi to Kim's place. Once more I was greeted with anger and disgust when I arrived to my girlfriend's apartment. Thankfully, the liquor running hot through my blood numbed me to the verbal attacks and abuse. An hour after my return, Kim calmed down and told me to lie next to her and the baby. She whispered one thing in my ear before dozing off, "No matter what and who you are, this is your baby. God allowed you to bless me with a child, and we will take care of him."

After she made that bold statement, she whispered to our baby boy Eliphalet, which means, *my God is deliverance*. She initially wanted to name him Tony because she said it was versatile, unisex. It was befitting of a gorgeous girl as well as a bodacious boy. I shared with her what the pastor told me he would be named, and encouraged her to name him my God is deliverance--Eliphalet.

So there I was, a complete family man, with an already dysfunctional family, but I had two people ready to love me unconditionally. I thought.

Daily Drama

Moving in with my girlfriend was more than an introduction to daily drama; it was the stage play for my new life. Day after day she would fuss about something. Everything I seemed to do for her and my baby boy was never enough. It was never enough money, although I was a broke college student. She was always suspicious of me, and I could understand why. Week after week Eliphalet would be crying. The fussing, complaining and crying was like a never ending roller coaster ride. Seemed like every day I opened the door to our apartment, I would get sick. Not only did I get sick of being around her, but I got depressed.

It was the first time in my life for everything and dealing with her drama was no exception. I didn't understand her at all. What did she really want me to do? I was there to take care of my son. I put food on the table, and I even made love to her from time to time. We were basically like a married couple without all the legal paperwork.

We decided to go to counseling to see why things were so bumpy between her and me. Upon entering the offices of Larry Peters, I felt at peace. With the wonderful oceanic paintings, and the whispers of the ocean's waves playing in the background, I was so comfortable, sleep almost found me during our first engagement. Larry Peters was a tall humble type of guy; he had to be at least six foot two inches with a lot of hair and a huge smile. We opened up our sessions in prayer, as Mr. Peters focused on the biblical answers in terms of relationships and the place of children in each relationship.

Thank God, his office had a daycare, I rarely wanted to see my baby boy out of my sight, let alone not be in the same building as he to hear his cries or screams if there was danger lurking. The best part about those sessions was the fact that I had an opportunity to open up about my past, my mistakes and my desires. Kim had a chance to dish out all of her dirt on me and past men that deceived her. She opened up to Mr. Peters and I about why she seemed to be so angry with me. And the one thing that I would never forget her saying is, 'you remind me of my father.'

She told Mr. Peters and I during our third visit all about her cheating father, how many woman he had when he and her mother was together, and she talked about all the promises he made with Kim and never kept. Kim had never told me what happened with her father till that day, never in a million years would I have known that the anguish against her father pitted a bad seed for me.

Mr. Peters just looked at the two of us like everything was normal during that third session, he quickly quoted some scripture in the bible, I believe it was Luke chapter twenty one verse sixteen and told us to come back and see him the following week.

Kim smiled; she was heavily enthused because she finally had a chance to release what was bothering her for years all in one session.

We went back for session four and discussed with Mr. Larry Peters everything from A to Z. he suggested for us to break up. Call it quits, put on the *see ya later* face. Of course my girlfriend and I were bitterly shocked, but looking at the facts, we weren't going to be able to sustain according to the way we were arguing. Mr. Peters made the bold suggestion for us to break up because of a few things, number one was morally. We were shacking and biblically that's wrong. Number two, well we just weren't happy with each other and the arguing was rather unhealthy for our child, and number three, the big enchilada, was the fact that I still had cravings for guys.

Three months later, my girlfriend and I did just that. We broke up, settled all of our evil conflicts and charged it to the game. Of course that wasn't the end of her, and surely not the end of my seeing my son. Four weeks later, she hit me with child support papers to sign. Four more weeks after that, funds were automatically being deducted from my employment checks. Four weeks following, my grades plummeted. Four weeks after my grades plummeted, I was back in a funky mode of depression and confusion. Four weeks later, I was in the arms of another man. Four weeks after falling into his arms, I moved in with him, because paying child support and rent on my own was adding up, not to mention the out-of-pocket cost of tuition.

Four weeks after moving in with my new man, he began some drama. He started with a mandate. I was not to see girls, including my baby's mama. Four weeks after he told me that, I finally had a chance to see my son. He was so precious, barely breaking one year. Four weeks after seeing my son, spring break arrived. I decided to go down to Miami to pay my family a visit. My baby mama reluctantly allowed me to take Eliphalet down there with me. Four weeks later I got into a fight at club Gomorrah, I will tell you about the fight a little bit later. They told me *I wasn't gay enough* to be there. I was terribly shocked and stupefied, trying to figure out how gay I had to be to go to a gay club?

Four weeks preceding the gay club incident, I received a phone call from my father that my mother had a mild stroke. Found out she'd been working overtime to support all of us, including sending me money from time to time. Both she and daddy were busting their butts, hustling day and night to provide for their offspring.

Four weeks after my mother had a stroke, the happenings of summer were in full swing. I decided to take summer off, again. I still managed to keep my G.P.A. at a 2.8 with all the drama, frustration and confusion polluting my life. Four weeks after summer began; I decided to move back out on my own. The guy I was living with was too controlling, not as bad as my baby mama, but still enough drama to make me sick as well.

Four weeks after moving out on my own, my grandmother died of cancer at the ripe old age of seventy-six. I flew back down to Miami to pay my respects to her. I loved that woman. She was definitely one of those big time spiritual folks.

My grandmother was in church Sunday to Sunday with the exception of Monday. Every time our family went to visit her she was always down on her knees slouched next to her favorite couch. When I said hello to grandma, she showed me her pearly white dentures and baited me in with a quick hug. Anyone just walking on the street couldn't tell that she was a grandmother, oh no, her hair was black as night and she kept a steady selection of fashionable clothing. If it wasn't for her bible toting self, I believe that she would have had more old geezers trying to holler at her than I've noticed.

I can recall the time I was in the mall with grandma looking for some school shoes at the age of eleven, two older looking gentleman who had to be in their seventies and she was in her sixties back then, they asked for her number. She said, "I'll give you a number alright, the area code is John 3:16 and the number is J-E-S-U-S." She had me screaming with laughter as I saw the two men look her up and down with disgust and left the same way they came, empty handed.

Yep, grandma was always fun to be around; she was the most religion I had when I was a kid. She was devastated by the incident with my uncle and I because he is her son, she didn't speak to him for a good year, but she chose to harness the power of forgiveness that she told so many people about and forgave him for what he'd done to me. That's one thing I could not do, as a matter of fact my grandmother and I had a few small arguments on the manner of forgiving my uncle for the crimes he'd done to me.

Now, grandma is gone and I guess she was right; life is too short to have hate on your heart. As a little boy she always told me, "folks just gone do things to make you mad, they gone do things to make you fear, when you let this sin thing get in the way, it can destroy a lot of what God intended for good. Baby, you are more than a conqueror, so let the Lord lead you to be the best man that you can be on a daily basis." I really miss her; I could really use some of that wisdom now.

Four weeks after the passing of my grandmother I was one month in the fall of my junior year in college. I was doing pretty good and Eliphalet was getting close to his terrible two's. At the same time, his body was maturing, and the doctors were still saying to wait before making a decision on his sexual organs because it was still too close to call. All the while I just observed his mannerisms whenever he was around me. In my opinion, he seemed more like the boy he was, than the extra female part he had. But just as the doctor ordered, we waited. Anxious. Can't-hardly-sleep-at-night anxious.

    Four months after talking to Eliphalet's doctor, spring break had come once more. During that spring break, I decided to take a trip to Cancun Mexico. In Cancun Mexico, two of my buddies and I were kidnapped and held at gun point for four weeks. It was not a pretty situation, to have absolutely no communication with family and friends, my buddies and I did not believe that we were going to make it out alive. I thought about all of my past successes and failures at least one-thousand times, I tried to put the pieces of the puzzle together as we sat there in this arid dungeon, with the stench of forty unseen dead dogs all at once. The smell alone would knock us out; I preferred the blows in the jaw than the stench of death all over us twenty-four seven.

    I have no idea why they kidnapped us, maybe they believed that we were rich coming from America, I did have on a little bling during the trip, but I didn't think it was that serious. Well,

I guess it is very serious when you are getting paid a bunch of pesos, which is not even close to the value of the American dollar. My buddies were livid, they were unsaved and gay. I thought that it would have been a great time to speak to them about Jesus Christ, but I felt like a hypocrite because we all were bed partners on the trip.

From our relationship in the states, my buddies knew that I had some connection with Christianity, but they didn't know how deep. In Mexico they saw me pray the way I saw my grandmother bend her knees to the floor. I wasn't a perfect Christian and I didn't want to die either. After the eight day of being placed in that *hell hole* my buddies gave their life to Christ, on the tenth day, they were on their knees praying with me. My time in Cancun, Mexico was a very life changing and humbling moment for me, the relationship with my buddies and with God drastically changed that day. No longer was I afraid to say who Jesus is, because it wasn't the Mexican police that rescued us that day, it was the love of Jesus who heard our cries and felt that we three homosexual men deserved another chance.

When I left for Cancun I weighed one-hundred and seventy pounds. When we were finally released I weighed one-hundred and forty pounds. The kidnappers barely fed us a crumb of bread and water.

Four months after that surreal incident in Mexico, I learned my son was making a lot of strides in his speech. I really understood what he was saying, and how he was saying it. Above all, he told me how he missed me, and how he loved me, and how he wished his mother and I would be together. He told me this over the phone when I got back from Mexico. Tears had immediately taken on their marching orders; I had no control over the wet molecules which streamed down my face and around my nose like the Jordan River.

Four months after the conversation with my son, I was trying on a cap and gown for my graduation. At the time, I couldn't believe how fast my senior year whizzed by at Francis State University, but it did. Four months after caps and gowns were fitted; I was walking across the stage once more. My whole family was there to see me and support me. Pictures, candid camera moments and good times with my family from Miami gave me so much to cheer about, especially since my incident in Mexico. Everyone was checking me out, my mother was asking if I had a disease because of all the weight I lost. I was happy to see that she was ok since suffering that stroke, but she looked fine to me, had all major functions operating in the right order. The doctor just told her to cut her hours down tremendously, stay away from pork and red meats while doing at least a mile a day to not only lower her cholesterol but also help as a stress reliever.

My son was getting bigger, and I was so happy that he and Kim was at the graduation.

Although the baby mama and I didn't quite get along, we'd learned to work things out for the good, especially when it came down to our heaven-sent son.

Four years later, I'm a water analyst for the City of Tallahassee. This brings me to my present day life. Enough about the past; it's time to live in the present, to better prepare for the future. Now my story must go on, and go on it will.

Part 2

"But now being made free from sin, and become servants to God, you have your fruit to holiness, and the end everlasting life."
                    Romans 6:22 K.J.V.

Out of the Club

"So Jesse, why do you have to keep tripping like this man? You know I got a son now man. I need to leave this life." I looked Jesse up and down as we argued outside of the pale brick building known as Club G. We loved to argue with one another; apparently Jesse gets turned on when we argue, I am turned off.

"Yeah, I heard about your two-parts son. He'll probably be a drag like you."

I slid my right hand across my face to wipe the little make up left from me sweating in the club inside. I leaned in to Jesse with my stilettos squeezing my feet to make sure I heard him correctly. My weave even feels like it's been partially sweated out, but no time to fix up my appearance, this man is talking about my son.

"Dude, those are fighting words. I can't believe you said that about my son. My son isn't going to be anything like me." *At least I hope not, I gave my self the head to toe look from my reflection in the car next to us. I immediately felt disgusted.*

"Did you mean your daughter?" Bam. Just like that, I hit Jesse in the jaw; his mouth is gushing with blood. It's probably the first time I hit somebody like that. *A person can talk about me however they feel, but don't talk about my son like that.*

"Why you had to hit me like that man?" Jesse replies with those tender, serious eyes which I fell so many times for.

"Because, dude, you crossed the line, you can talk about me, but when it comes down to my family, I don't take any prisoners." His blood is still streaming onto the sidewalk; luckily the music is so loud, that the security personnel did not have time to come over to hear what was going on. I felt bad now, but I'm not going to tell him that.

"But you know I'm telling the truth." Jesse insisted on trying me, he backed up three inches, just enough to touch the grass on the property and escape another potential blow to the nose.

"You say one more word, Jesse, and your brains will be served up in my bowl for spaghetti! I'm serious man. Let it go. Eliphalet and his mom are going up to the doctor's in a few weeks to get it fixed. It ain't his fault he was born that way. He didn't choose to be this.

Thinking about my little Eli, I wouldn't trade him for the world. It's a blessing to have seen him teeth, to eat his first meal, to catch his first words and even to see his poop. They are all blessings which God gave to Kim and I, and from the day he was born with the problem, we knew that he would be something special. My son is a genius, he earns all A's in school, and he just loves everybody.

"Ok, ok man. Stop tripping. Besides, when you and I gone see each other again?" The blood subsided, his shirt was painted with blood, and his jeans suffered a few dots of red as well.

"The answer is never, dude. Its time for me to do something positive with my life, and meeting guys at Club G ain't helping me." *This is going to be tough, but I can do it.*

"Are you serious dawg? Dawg, you in a trap cousin. Listen to yourself, Paul. You're gay. You love men. You'll always be gay; there is no way out. I tried to walk the straight line before. Guess what it got me? It got me sleeping with more dudes than when I first started out. I'm telling you man, this is the life." He shook his head as he patted his right pants pocket to make sure his car keys were there. He dug into his left pants pocket and found the keys to his red 2010 Honda Accord. We both cautiously walked over to his car, I parked just a few cars to the right of him.

His words sting like the bite bestowed upon a praying mantis after making love to his mate. Jesse's words resound in my ear. You're gay. You love men. This I cannot deny. I had loved Brian, loved Dave. But I had also loved Sandra, though I was young. Puppy love is still love, nonetheless. Indeed I loved Kim too, for she had given me a son. A son! That's it! That's my defense. I love my son more than anything in the world. I'd do anything; give up anything to give him a better life. It reminds me of another father who did almost exactly the same. He gave up something, someone, a part of himself to make sure all his children would have a better life. I could not imagine giving up Eliphalet to the snares of this world. I know what to say, now.

"This is the life for some, yeah. But by the power and blood of Jesus Christ, this is not the life for me. Yeah I was sexually abused when I was a kid, yeah I do things with men, but I refuse to live my life this way, especially now that I got a kid.

Tell me this, Jesse, what are the kids at his school going to say? 'Look at his gay father; he's probably gay too.' I don't want my son to go through that. Listen man, I want this freedom for myself. I know it's going to be a lot of hard work, but I'm willing to make the necessary sacrifices to get my life completely right with God. I want to be free from this so-called trap. I don't want to turn anymore. I want God, and I want out."

"You go ahead Kesha, Paul, whatever name you like to go by undercover. But you hear this one thing about God: God loves us all. You hear me man. God loves us all. Doesn't matter whether we're gay, straight, Muslim or Christian, God loves us all. So, I'm good homey. I'm good"

"You're right Jesse, God does love us all. Why wouldn't He? He created us, right? But I've come to find out that it's not a matter of Him not loving us; it's a matter of Him not loving the sins we commit. And as far as what I've read, if you and I don't get our acts together, we both got us a first class ticket to hell!"

"Since when did you become a preacher?" Jesse looks at me with blatant astonishment.

"Since God's been preaching to me, showing me my wrongs and constantly telling me what I need to do to get my life right."

"Alright sucka, I don't have time to hear this, I'm out of here."

"Alright Jesse, get some band-aids for that womb, you're going to need it buddy."

The Death of Jesse

The choir is singing "Amazing Grace", the elders in the back are crying, Jesse's mother is screaming and having convulsions all over the place. It seems as if it is a scene taken right out of the movies. The services are being held at The Truth Baptist Church which is approximately five miles from the church I attend; it's the only *gay friendly* church in Tallahassee.

I visited The Truth Baptist Church a few times, but it was hard to feel comfortable there, because everybody that was at Club G on Saturday night was at church on Sunday morning. Part of me felt that this church was just an extension of the club; the people danced and talked the same way. Common sense also told me that there was no truth at Truth Baptist Church, because how could God destroy a whole city for the type of lifestyle that many of the so called saints are living at Truth Baptist. I know I got my skeletons, but at least I'm working towards being better, many of those punks that attend Truth Baptist, well let's just say that they don't want to change, and they try to find every scripture in the bible to justify their sins.

From the rainbow colored walls to the light pink halls, The Truth Baptist church has taken on a style of its own, now even I can't complain about that. This back row seating feels mighty empty when you don't know anybody, all the wailing, all the crying will not bring Jesse back to us again. Let's just hope that these same folks in here won't be the friends he see in *hell*!

Two weeks after the whole fight incident Jesse and I had, Jesse was pronounced dead at Tallahassee Memorial Hospital. I'll never forget the phone call I received from the hospital. Jesse had listed me as next to kin, along with his mother. The nurse on the other end of the line asked me to come in. I had no idea what was going on, but I hoped Jesse was okay, in spite of the dispute we had. When I arrived to the hospital, Jesse's mother was already there, in Jesse's room, seated beside his lifeless body. I entered the room slowly, almost tip-toeing. I stopped inches away from his mother's back and placed my hand gently on her shoulders. She turned and looked at me. The deep wrinkles in her face were scars, I knew, from years of worrying. My mother had begun to develop those same wrinkles. Her eyes looked as dry as a clay pot roasting in a furnace. Her delicate hands trembled as she placed the drenched, embroidered handkerchief to her face to catch the falling drops. No doubt the wave of tears was triggered by thoughts of her only son, her lost son. I stepped in closer, embraced her with my hug. I could not imagine losing Eliphalet to the snares of this world, I thought. I, too, began to tremble with tears.

After identifying the corpse as Jesse Parker I learned that he officially died from pneumonia, linked to his conception of the A.I.D.S. virus. Jesse had full blown A.I.D.S. and I didn't even know. I couldn't tell by looking at him, and of course I didn't think to ask at the time.

Jesse's mother told me she didn't know about the disease either. We're not even sure if Jesse knew. Wow, all we know about Jesse was the fact that he was dead at the age of thirty-two. The man still had some life left to live in him.

I took my A.I.D.S test the same week of finding out how Jesse died. I should be getting my results a few days after the funeral, which is progressing rather slowly. I think it's because Jesse's mom is taking the loss of her son very hard. The ushers run to her side at every convulsing episode, even while the minister is giving the eulogy. I continue watching from where I am seated. Though my body is present, my mind is distant. Many questions cross my mind as I think of Jesse's body lying lifeless in the navy blue casket. The flower arrangements blanketing the alter where the casket stood. The first question that crosses my mind is, why did he have to die so soon? Then I ask myself did he catch that first flight to hell, or did someone meet him on the way to convince him about heaven? As the pastor once said: Its' only through Jesus Christ that we are able to see God. Either way, it is quite difficult to get any answers out of Jesse considering he is dead, his body without a soul.

I'm glad I alerted Kim and told her the situation. Telling her about Jesse's death and his cause of death was one of the hardest things I've had to do since I was born.

Back at the hospital, when they lulled Jesse's body out of the room, I dashed into the hallway, paced the floor. I was nervous; my stomach was upset because I knew I needed to tell Kim. I ran to the nearest restroom, found a vacant stall, and threw up. I did this until I was empty inside. Empty of emotions that kept me from telling Kim the truth. Finally, exhausted, I exited the stall. I stumbled to the sink and splashed some cool water on my face. Then, I left the bathroom and caught the elevator to the first floor. The chapel was on the first floor. Once inside the chapel, I pulled my cell phone from my pocket, strolled through my address book, and stopped on the name that read Kim. I called. The phone rang twice.

"Hello?"

"Kim," I cleared my throat, dry, itchy.

"Yeah, this is she. Paul? You don't sound so good. Is everything alright?"

"I hope so," I chuckled. I guess I did so to keep from crying, again. I needed to be strong. To be a man at this very moment in my life. "I'm at the hospital."

"Oh my goodness! Paul? Why didn't you tell me? I can be there in thirty minutes. I just need to get Eliphalet dressed."

"No need for all of that. It's not me. I'm fine," I paused. "It's Jesse." I could tell she had no idea who I was talking about because I only heard her slightly breathing through the silence. "Jesse is...was..." I continued to tell her all about Jesse, all about his situation, all about our fight.

She was angry, scared altogether. But she took the test and is waiting on her results as well. I think she should be cool, though, because I didn't have sex with her in a while.

I feel so sad and afraid right now. All the things I have been through with Jesse and the last thing I could remember was punching him in the face. I guess there's just something a small band-aid can't prevent, especially when it comes down to A.I.D.S.

As my mind continues to wonder, I am interested in knowing exactly what does a person with A.I.D.S. really look like, how can someone tell? I search the faces of the individuals in the church. Any one of them could have it. Including me.

I didn't notice the minister had concluded his sermon. As the pastor said one last prayer over Jesse's dead body, I reminisce on all the people who went up before him to give their testimonials. There were all these different people who I had never seen before talking about how good of a person Jesse was. My inward man is crying, crying because I know that this homosexual lifestyle is wrong, and there's nothing good about it.

If good can't get me into heaven, then I don't want *good* at all. I want what I see the people in church wanting. I want who they call the *King of Kings* and the *Lord of Lords*. I want Jesus! *I'm dying to be straight!*

The pastor gives the benediction and the congregation joins in the recession. Limousines and Chevy's head to the graveyard; one by one we follow each other to the place where we all will rest some day. For now we have an ounce of breath, and with this time we must use it before we lose it.

"Hey son, yeah, you son over there. How do you know Jesse?" As discrete as I am trying to be, some old fart is still calling out to me.

"Jesse and I were friends. We go back a while." I tell the old man.

"Were you practicing the funny too?" His face is worn with malice.

I can tell this guy doesn't have any sense. Instead of being straight up with me like a man, he wants to beat around the bush.

"You mean was I practicing homosexuality, sir?"

"Yeah, yeah that's right son. Did you play with more than your pee-pee?" He gives me a stern glance, but as far as I'm concerned, this guy is a joke and very rude. But I'll go ahead and answer the old man.

"I don't think it should concern you as to what I do in the bedroom. I don't recall asking you if the blue pill was good enough for you. I mean, with all due respect old man, everyone here knows the lifestyle of a homosexual. I don't have to break it down to you like I was talking to my son."

"Oh Lord, you got a son too. And you playing with him as well I bet."

Alright, he has crossed the line. I don't care how old this grandpa is, he is about to catch a beat down. But before I could reach my hand out to injure his jaw, Jesse's mother gets between us and says she wants to talk to me.

"So you sure you don't mind talking to me in private over there?" Jesse's mother asks me.

"Of course not." We walk over to a little bench a few feet away.

Teary eyed and in despair she says to me, "So what was he like?"

"What do you mean?" I kind of knew what she meant, but couldn't quite comprehend it.

"I mean Jesse, what was he like?"

"He was cool, hot headed, and like a good friend." I notice her nervousness and pain ridden eyes.

"Sounds like my Jesse. The boy had a temper from the day he was born. Don't really sound like he changed a bit."

"Well I guess not ma'am."

"You know Jesse rarely came to visit us in North Carolina. I had to practically pay the boy to come to see me, even when I was ill. Who could blame him though, his father practically disowned him, and his family rebuked the *hell* out of him. I guess if I was him, I wouldn't have wanted to come around them old folks either. "

"I know what you mean, ma'am. I know what you mean."

"All these people come down here to Tallahassee to say good words about my boy now that he's dead. They ain't never said hardly two good words about him while he was alive. Seemed to me that they committed a worse sin than homosexuality, and that sin was a lack of love for your kin folk, in spite of their...differences.

Seems like the only time you can get folks to love each other are on Easter and Christmas and during weddings and funerals. But when all the dust settles and the scraps of chicken bones are thrown away, I declare this today; things will never be the same with my baby gone. But you knew him. You were probably the closest thing to him.

He told me about that little fight yawl got into. I knew something was the matter when he called me early the next morning. It'd been months since I last heard from him. Anyway, something you said to him that night before must have really eaten away at his conscience. He said he could hardly sleep because he'd gotten in an argument with a good friend of his." She looks at me, my head held down. With one hand, she cups mine in hers. With the other hand, she lifts my chin. Her eyes pierce the windows to my soul. Child I forgive you. He was hurt, but he understood he hurt you too by talking about your family."

She gently releases her hands from holding mine and frees my chin. Her fragile hands are folded once again in her lap, atop another one of her embroidered handkerchiefs. My eyes follow the floral designs etched in thread. The handkerchief exhibits magnificent detail, down to the very lace that edges the cloth. During the brief moment of silence between us, I remember the magnificent detail God designed each of our lives with. Like the thread on an embroidery cloth, such is our lives.

"Are you saved young man?" Breaking the silence, she twitched her nose nervously about how I would respond. "Well you ought to know that this life is not the life for you. Jesus has another plan for you, and Jesus saved my boy Jesse right before he died. Jesse received salvation right at that hospital with the same pastor who buried him." She points a bony finger toward the guy wearing a low fade, reading glasses, a black cloak that nearly reached his ankles, black trousers, and black dress shoes. He looks morbid.

"There was something you told Jesse that night that burdened him," she continues, "because he was confused and mentioned you talked a lot about God." She bows her head with a hint of shamefulness, "Jesse told me he'd be on his death bed and still not accept Christ in his life. He told his father he'd rather make his bed in hell than to fool with two-faced Christians in heaven."

I divert my attention from the morbid pastor offering condolences to the bereaved. "That sounded like me a while ago, but things have become different for me ever since my baby boy was born. I know that everything happens for a reason, even this very conversation we're having. I also know, ma'am that we have a choice, and I'm choosing to believe that I can change."

"Yes my love, you can change, for whoever the Son sets free, is truly free indeed. You will be delivered from that strong hold. Now give your mother a hug," she slightly shifted her body to face me and extended her feeble arms. "Come on, don't be shy. There's nothing like the love of a mother, or any other woman; don't let the devil fool you into thinking otherwise. We women know stuff and can do stuff that no man can do, starting with giving birth.

Jesse was my only child. Now you're the closest person I have to remember him by. Take care of your family son, and let God use you in an extraordinary way. You hear me?"

"Yes ma'am I hear you." I accept her embrace. Her love covers me like no other love I have felt before. I hug her back with all my might, basking in the moment. I am delighted to hear that my words struck a nerve in her son, my friend, Jesse. While on his death bed, he accepted Jesus Christ into his life. He isn't lost after all. He's been found. My eyes swell with joy; my lids cannot contain the flood; my cup runneth over.

"Always remember now, there's nothing too hard for God, and give me a call sometimes, ok." She pats my back.

"Alright, I will," I sob. I try to suck up my tears as we untie our arms from around each other. I gave her a quick smile and left the site unnoticed. I was free from the hypocrites, naysayers and verbal slayers.

The Life of Jesus

There is nothing more tormenting about going to the doctor's office than to have to sit there amongst the slush pile of old magazines, smell the stench of three and four year old children, while continuing to hear the old ladies ask the same questions. This office would look a lot better if I did not have to wait thirty minutes to see the doctor, I mean, in a world of texting and tweeting, why can't they just text me the results, at least while driving I could let my anger or happiness out on the open road. No, I have to wait. Ok. The cheesy artwork he has posted up in the waiting room is beginning to annoy me. It's too cold in here, who controls the temperature? Not another hutchie mama coming thru, I bet she comes in for a test every week.

"Mr. Stringer." A pretty Caucasian woman with dingy looking scrubs approaches me.

"Finally," I muttered under my breath, as the Goosebumps began to accelerate from the cold air and fear. What could possibly be wrong with me, I'm perfectly healthy, maybe I should turn back now before the doctor says that I was crazy for coming here.

"Have a seat right here; the doctor will be with you shortly." She smiled; she was pretty, but nothing original about her. She had that nine to five type smile, you know the kind that says that I'm just smiling because my boss tells me to, but wait till after five, I'll be another animal. Yeah. That was her.

Five minutes later the doctor shows up, coincidentally, he wasn't the same doctor that administered the test, but he was here to give me the news. What's up with that? He might have read the test wrong; he wasn't in the room when I was sweating profusely on the day I took the test. I hope he has good insurance, because if there is anything I find wrong with him or this office, I'm suing.

"I'm sorry to tell you this, Mr. Stringer," Oh no, sorry, already. This guy is blunt; he could at least give me the sugar before the water. "But you are H.I.V. positive," the doctor says as everything seems to go in slow motion. I collapse on the floor of his office.

"Call the nurse in here, call the nurse in here at once," the doctor remains calm and knows exactly what to do with me. The doctor administers some sort of sedative to bring me back and well, I appreciate that, but I'd rather be passed out right now.

Yep, here I am, looking up at the ceiling just like Jesse. The only difference between him and me is that he's already dead. As the nurse checks my pulse, I easily clear one-hundred and seventy blood pressure. My heart is racing fast, and my mind is moving slow. All I can think about is the nearest gun shop. Since I'm going to die anyway, I might as well get it done sooner than later.

As my mind speeds up, catches up to reality, I stand up on my two feet, then immediately sit back down at attention. The doctor looks at me all confused, wondering if I am going to repeat another collapse. He tells me about all the medical arrangements and medical jargon and states that by law, they had to automatically report me to the Center for Disease Control, as if I was some abandoned pet with rabies. Everything the doctor said seemed to go in one ear and out the other. The only thing that seems more real to me is the fact that he told me I had H.I.V.

"So son, come back here in six months, and we'll see if there are any changes in your future results. In the meantime, please stay away from risky sexual behaviors and remember to alert all of the partners that you've been with in the last ten years about your disease. Try not to scare them, but as a word of precaution, they just may want to get tested."

"Ok, ok doctor," I read the name on his white lab coat, "Evolsidog, but is there any other hope for me now that I've got this disease?"

"You know son, I've never been a religious man and could care less about the way religion is taught to people. But, if I had to say something as a glimmer of hope for your situation, I noticed a miracle happen in the lives of this young couple who were trying to have a son. I told them every reason why they wouldn't have a child, test after test came up negative for child birth. I told them that the best option for them was adoption because having natural born children of their own was not an option.

Week in and week out they would come in to see if my medical diagnostic was still the same, but little did I know that between those visits here they were praying, they were praying for a miracle baby. None of my medical expertise or medications was any match with the miracle that took place in their lives.

That young, humble, patient and beautiful couple welcomed a healthy baby boy into their family. I was actually in the delivery room with them. On the day of the birth, I asked them what did they know that I didn't know about child birth? They told me emphatically that they simply knew Jesus. My eyes lit up like a child being sung too.

And that wasn't the only unexplained miracle to ever happen here, but that miracle of their son's birth was a wonderful miracle, and it truly was the first miracle that stood out to me."

"So, are you suggesting that I pray for a miracle?"

"Yes indeed son, yes indeed." Doctor Evolsidog disappears around the corner with a flutter of his stone white coat.

How could I let this happen to me? I thought I used the right steps to keep myself protected, at least most of the times.

"Church folks I need you to understand that God is an awesome God. He sent down his only Son to save us and show us an example of what we ought to be as people. No matter the trial, no matter the tribulations or the sickness, Jesus can save you.

Jesus can even save you from crack cocaine, A.I.D.S. and prostitution. You don't believe me, just flip through God's word and there's plenty of proof there."

The pastor is preaching a sermon which seems like it was handpicked from God specifically for me. I'm just having a hard time believing how I'm going to be healed from one of the world's deadliest diseases.

"Now listen folks, you've got to fast, and you've got to pray. Folks, you got to lay it all out there on the line for Jesus. There shouldn't be anyone or anything before him. No television, no computer, no sports, no school, and even your wife is to not come before him. It's by the blood of Jesus saints that all things are made possible."

I'm feeling the pastor and I'm sort of not feeling the pastor. I'm confused, upset, depressed and really don't know where to start.

The doctor already has me taking about eight different medications each day for the rest of my life. Before discharging me, the doctor said the importance for me taking these medications is simply for me to live longer. But why live longer? What's the purpose? What? Does he just want me to spread the disease to someone else for as long as I live? Why live longer in humiliation and shame? What am I going to tell my parents? My son? Living longer sounds like a great option, but not when it destroys everyone else along the way. I hate my life. I hate my choices. I'm a failure, a punk, a dead man walking.

If I'm going to feel better and do better, I need to want it for myself. This time there will be no backsliding, no mistakes, just time to move toward perfection, and a love that I can call my own in the name of Jesus Christ!

"Do I have any believers out there who believe in miracles?" The pastor continues with his long-winded sermon. "Folks, tell your neighbors next to you that you believe in miracles. Go ahead, don't be shy. Say it like you mean it." The pastor shouts, his voice echoing all throughout the pews in the back, where I'm sitting.

"I believe in miracles," I say to a young girl about my age who is my closest neighbor, but I wasn't really sure if I really believed it—what I said.

"Turn with me in your bibles to the book of Matthew, chapter one, verse twenty-three. I'll be reading from the King James Version. And it says: 'Behold a virgin shall be with child and shall bring forth a son, and they shall call his name Immanuel, which being interpreted is, God with us.' Now, I'm going to stop right there, because that's a miracle in itself ladies and gentleman. Listen to this. Mary, oh Mary, was about to have a baby while she's yet a virgin. I said she's a virgin ya'll," he wails. The congregation hoops and screams at the pastor's remarks. "But here's the real kicker folks, not only is Mary about to have a baby, but it's God in the flesh, the same God who created Mary, and you," he points in all directions, "and you and you! It's God, ya'll, it's God. Hallelujah, hallelujah, thank you God for Jesus! "

One thing about a good early Sunday morning preaching, you will get some hoops, hollers and enough noise to put the Roosters out of business.

"I have something to be thankful for this morning; God performed a miracle on that young Virgin Mary. Thank you Jesus. Amen." The pastor put some whip cream on top of this sermon. "Now listen here folks, turn around and tell your neighbor, God has already performed the miracle because he's always here with me."

"God has already performed the miracle because he's here with me." This time I'm speaking to the old granny sitting behind me.

"Church, church the life of Christ, Jesus Christ that is, is one of great miracles, long suffering and even exposure to great temptation. But through His righteousness, His love for each one of us and perseverance, He made the ultimate sacrifice. Folks, let me ask you this: Have you ever sacrificed anything for anybody? If so, when was the last time you did so?

The church done got quiet 'round here; don't let me preach to myself. Don't get me wrong, I've done my wrongs and share with you in some of my selfish tendencies, but putting all excuses aside, Jesus sacrificed his life. We make up every excuse to not sacrifice two hours of our time a month to volunteer at the homeless shelter. So I assume that would be a miracle for you, a miracle for you to get to the homeless shelter and make it to both sessions of church.

Jesus walked on water; we can't even walk on the sidewalk. Come on fellow Christians and you non-believers in the building, we all got to do better than the way we present ourselves. If we expect many miracles and signs and wonders, we have to put in our time with the Lord. We have to put in our time with the Prince of Peace. He's already got our checks ready and waiting for heaven, but too many of us keep deducting the balance off of it, putting your account on hold.

Jesus Christ did some amazing things when he walked this Earth in the full body of man. When are you going to start thinking like Jesus and believing that amazing things can happen with you too? "

Right then I remembered. Jesus came to me that day, that day that I was in middle school. The only thing that went wrong since then is the fact that I wasn't man enough to come to him like He has come to me. I kept pushing him back, pushing him away, now my life is on the line, and I really see that I need him now more than ever.

"And saints before I finish this sermon, I'd like to say one more thing." I sort of hear and don't hear the pastor exclaiming. "Who can know us better than God does? Who can know our faults, our secrets, our mess-ups better than God does? Nobody, nobody but Jesus, for Jesus Christ is Lord! And he shall be Lord over all of our lives.

Saints if you need a miracle, if you need your head to be anointed by the oil, if you need salvation, come to the altar. Come to the altar. Please come to the altar, for God will make everything alright. Come you, come here now. The sooner you believe, the sooner you'll be set free. Do you hear me? Do you hear me saints?"

"Pastor I hear you. I need a miracle!" I scream from the top of my lungs. I could hold it in no longer. The pain in my voice erupted from a place deep within me.

"Well come on up then brother. The Lord is in the miracle-working business."
I run on up like I did the last time, feeling a move of the Lord. At least that's what the elder folks call it, a move from the Lord.

"Son, what do you need the Lord to heal you of today?"

"I need the Lord to heal me of H.I.V., and also I need the Lord to turn me away from homosexuality, one of my partners just died of A.I.D.S. and I am so afraid. I'm afraid to die." At this point, I am not ashamed. I don't care what people may think of me. Their thoughts can't be any worse than what they already think of me. Besides, I am desperate.

"Well, are you saved son?"

"Yes sir, I'm saved." I vigorously shake my head.

"Well son," the pastor sternly glances at me, "you shouldn't be afraid of death, because Jesus has already broken its power. And at His return, the keys to Hades will be destroyed for good. No more crying, no more dying, just a peace with the father God and his son Jesus.

Now, as far as that H.I.V. is concerned, you ever heard of the woman with the issue of blood?" He moves a little closer to me.

"No sir." I look at him with sweat gliding from my face. *I thought that all women had an issue with blood.*

"Well, this particular, peculiar woman had some blood issues, some can say similar to A.I.D.S., Lupus, Sickle Cell or whatever blood diseases that we presently struggle with. But I tell you this son: That woman went down on her knees with such a humble gesture of faith and touched the hem of Jesus' garment. When that woman touched his garment, she was immediately healed because of her faith. So, if God can dry up and destroy her issue of blood, He surely can do it for you. Not to say that it's instantly going to happen right now because he works on His time and may want you to learn something. But God will heal you of this disease if you believe and trust in Him.

"Yes sir I believe," I say, my heart beating in fear and with aspirations for a healing.

"Now son, as far as this confusion of your liking men, well, that's nothing but a trick of the enemy. God never ever intended a man to be with another man nor a woman with another woman. If that was the case, my friend, how would we be able to procreate? That is a lying, deceiving spirit over your life and I rebuke that demonic homosexual spirit in the name of Jesus Christ!" The pastor lifts my hands high above my head, anoints my head with oil. I feel a strong, calloused hand against my forehead. It is definitely a hand that has had its share of rebuking demons, I imagine. I close my eyes as he begins to pray: "Lord I pray that you give this young man a true desire for women. Take away any lust and strong hold for men. Lead him on a path of righteousness; help him to be straight.

Heal his body, Lord Jesus. Show him that the victory lies with you and remind him that whoever the son sets free is truly free indeed. Thank you, Jesus. Thank you, Jesus!" the pastor proclaims. "Father God we thank you. We praise you; we magnify you and glorify your name. In Jesus' name," he pushes his rough hands harder against my forehead as if he was trying to force out all ill manner of thinking, "we give you all the glory and the honor. Amen!"

"Amen," I repeat.

"Now son," he continues, "there's one more thing. Have you heard about the man that was healed of the demons that possessed his soul? There were thousands of demons in that man, and the man was literally on the verge of suicide. Have you heard about that son?

"No sir," I say once more, shaking my head. Indeed, I hardly know much about anybody in the Bible. I guess I need to start reading it more. I still did not recognize the curious faces that are behind me, either judging me or praying earnestly for me.

"Well the bottom line to the story is the fact that Jesus cast out the legion of demonic spirits that had been living in that man, torturing him day and night, and the spirits went into the pigs nearby. The pigs then drowned themselves in the nearby water supply. Jesus told his disciples, 'These come out through fasting and praying.' Son, you need to do some fasting, some praying, and I mean some heavy duty praying. Not any now-I-lay-me-down-to-sleep praying. You need to lie prostrate before the Lord and seek his face. Cry out to him. Get closer to Him, so close that you can reach out and touch his garment. You understand?" he asks.

I nod.

"Also, you need to get in the Bible and read Genesis to Revelations."

I nod again.

Backing away from me, he makes room for the members of the special needs ministry to carry me away. "Can someone from the special needs ministry please come up and escort this young man to the back for counseling?" He looks in the direction of the ministerial corner. "God loves you son," he assures as I am swooped away, "a miracle is on the way," he tells me. "My time is up folks. Let's give God a hand clap of praise for what he's done; what he's doing, and what he will continue to do. Praise God for moving in such a powerful way this morning. Come on up, Deacon Combs, and finish up the church business."

As one of the ministers placed his arm around my shoulder, emphasizing that Jesus loves me, all I can think about is the last words the pastor spoke to me. *A miracle is on the way.* He didn't say that a miracle may happen; he said that a *miracle is on the way!* I pray that it comes soon enough. I pray that it comes before it's too late.

Dying

My baby mama got her results back; they are negative for the disease. As for my son, his medical procedure went well. The surgeon was careful and precise. Now Eliphalet is finally the boy that he was meant to be. I'm very happy that he was born. I mean, it's not like he was growing breasts or anything, he just had a temporary deformity where his unmentionables happen to be located.

As for me, I'm sick, I have the common cold but I'm alright for now. I guess the effects of being H.I.V. Positive hasn't kicked in to full gear yet. Apparently, I still have a pretty healthy white blood cell count. This means I can still get the common cold and not die from it. Besides that I recently landed a gig with the City of Tallahassee as a water analyst, work has been awfully stressful lately. We've been clocking in overtime to keep the sewage from the freshwater. A bad storm came in and did some heavy duty damage to our drainage systems.

Besides a stressful job, an upset (but forgiving) baby mama, a happy son, and a cold, everything else seems to be fine. I'm so used to having someone to talk to. A partner to play around with or a movie to go see with a group of friends. But ever since Jesse died, and I have had to call each and every partner I have ever fooled around with to inform them about my disease.

Consequently, life has been very different for me on the social side of things. The friends that I use to associate with don't want to be around me anymore since they found out that I am H.I.V. positive. Kim tries to keep me as far away from Eli as she could in fear that H.I.V. has all of a sudden become an airborne disease. Things are just not the same, especially without Jesse. Does this mean I'll never have friends? Does this mean that I'll never be able to make true love to someone ever again? "God if you hear me," I stop whatever I am doing, whatever I am thinking, to speak with the Father for just a moment, "I'm dying; I'm dying a slow death. Please God will you help me get my life back?"

I believe even God has to get tired of us, sooner or later, doing the same old thing over and over again, but expecting a different result. But he had warned me; he had certainly warned me many times. Yet I refused to change. Now that I'm on my death bed, I expect a miracle from Him? How ludicrous. Now I expect him to just jump at my command, my plea. While all the while, I did not obey his commands. I shake the thought of being miraculously healed away from my mind once again. Wow! My life is so screwed up, even the devil is probably laughing in my face, pointing the finger at me.

As I think and ponder on all the things I have done, all I can ask is what if? What if I hadn't gone to such and such's house? What if I didn't go to such and such club? What if my baby mama didn't get pregnant? Don't get me wrong, I am at the absolute happiest with my son, nurturing him, training him up so that he will not stray. I love that boy to death. I cannot imagine losing him to the snares of this world. I'm just thinking long, steady and hard about all of this mess that I put myself through. When you're down, you're down. Right now I feel as down as Pinocchio's nose when he's telling the truth.

I feel about as down as the dirt settling in my backyard. I feel about as down as an old hunchback man walking around with a cane, the hunchback of Tallahassee. I *feel* about as down as a preacher who couldn't preach a good service to save his soul. I feel as down... you know what? Let me end it all right now; down be damned. Be gone! Maybe I should kill myself, right here, right now. I have survival pills galore; I could easily overdose. I don't have a rifle, but I have a draw full of knives. Perhaps I can take a long, hot, steaming bath. Submerge myself in its wet embrace. I'm desperate, desperate to get this whole thing over with now. Nobody loves me anyway. Who could love a homo—former or not—with H.I.V.? After all, "He brought this upon himself," I can hear them gossiping. People don't call me like they used to, either. Logically, committing suicide will keep me from hurting anyone else or at least from giving them the disease.

Life sucks. It really does suck! It's not my fault about what happened with my uncle. I was too young to truly understand any of it. It's not my fault, Lord. He was evil. The devil used him to hurt me, to hurt the ones I love, to curse my offspring. Why? Why, God, did bad things have to happen to me? Is this to teach me some sort of lesson? Because if so, I get it. I get it now. I really, really get it.

Father God, why have you forsaken me? I was only a little boy, you could have stopped him. Yes, you! This is your fault!

My emotions are like hot lava oozing from a volcano now. The tears splotch my shirt. I can't remember what I was doing before my outburst. I don't know where I am.

As I continue to contemplate suicide, though, I come to the conclusion that death by my own hand ain't even worth it. Yeah, life seems bad, but death seems worse. Suicide represents a loss of faith in God, a loss in the belief that he will deliver me from my addictions and from my disease. So here I stand, faithful and in prayer that some sort of miracle will happen for me.

Right now I'm dying, the H.I.V. is slowly but surely bringing me to my demise, but I'm also dying to be straight. I would be stupid to go down with this disease without a fight. Yeah, it may have thrown me a left hook, right hook and maybe even a jab. But in the end of all things, I'm throwing some back. I can't sit here like it's all over because the pastor told me to believe in miracles.

After hours of nearly killing myself and pointing the finger at God, I decided that it would be best that I take a quick trip to see the people who mean the most to me in my life right now. Of course that is my son and his mother. I'm not going to call over there because I already know how she would respond; I'm just simply going by the apartment to make a surprise visit. Hopefully she doesn't go crazy when she sees me unexpectedly.

"Paul, your son does not need to see you like this." Kim states with grave concern. Eliphalet is standing right behind her listening to our conversation. He's mute, but I can see him.

"Like what? I'm straight girl; it ain't like I'm about to die today. Besides, the doctor said I got like a few years before it turns into full blown A.I.D.S."

"All I'm saying is that I don't want our son growing up thinking about his sick father who died!"

"Sweetie, sweetie," I sing "I'm good; I'm trusting and depending on God that I'll get better."

"Well you should have trusted and depended on him when you were bending over.

While you were bending over you should have been praying, not playing around with men like Jesse."

"Listen, Listen, I don't have time for this," I moan. She's mad at me now. But I don't care. How could she say such a foul thing, especially at a time such as this when my spirit has hit rock bottom and my soul needs healing. Why does she even have to bring up stuff like this? "What I did in the confines of my bedroom is my business," I rebut. "What you did with whoever is your business. You talking like you never bent over before."

"Yeah, that's how we got Eliphalet." She smacks her lips. "Shoot, I should have known your type from the moment you asked me to let you get if from behind. One of my sister girls warned me that when a man wants to make love in forbidden places that he's either gay or a super, super freak," she whines. "Obviously you're gay!"

"You know what baby girl, I'm out of here. I can't even have a decent conversation with my son's mother without her bringing up the past," I conclude. "I bet, I bet if I had a camera taping every wrong you've done, you'd turn off the tape within the first five minutes of my replaying it."

"So, don't act like my wrongs are worse than your wrongs. All sins are treated the same." I chuckle as I see her demeanor change from innocent to straight up stupid.

"Ok, Paul, you won. Are you happy now?" She frowns.

"Yep, I'm extraordinarily happy," I cheese from temple to temple.

"That's good, because I'm leaving, and Eliphalet is going with me."

"But...and where are you going?"

"I'm going to a friend's house. Stop bugging. I'm going to have a real man, not one that's half and half like the cream in my coffee. I need a real man to help me raise my son, a real father figure. All I'm saying is you can't be half and half, Paul; you got to be a real man all the way."

"First of all, I am a real man that deals with *real man issues;* there are more people in the world, not just me, who have had struggles with homosexuality."

"Well I wouldn't just call them struggles, Paul. I'd prefer to call them addictions. You are addicted to men."

"No, I'm not." I whined.

"Yes you are." She's being insistent.

"No, I'm not!" Now I know a full blown argument is on the way.

"Yes you are!" She insists again. She's about to piss me off.

"Ok, this conversation is going nowhere." I yell at her.

"Say goodbye to your son, Paul."

"Goodbye son, hope you're getting better treatment than this."

"What you said?" The gravity took on her face as she mean mugged me.

"You heard me. I didn't stutter. You basically have been treating me like crap. Let the past be past and the future be pleasant," I mention, hoping she cools down.

"You're right. That's why you're in my past. And uh…wait a second buddy, you're expecting me to just back down and act like you didn't put me at a high risk for the disease you're harboring in your blood stream and all your bodily secretions. You've got to be kidding me, Paul. You could have given me H.I.V. you faggot. I could have given it to my son." Her selfish words strike a nerve. He's my son, too.

She continues her rant. "I mean, what were you thinking? What was I thinking? Oh wait, I know. I was thinking that I had me a real man." she hisses. "You ain't nothing but a wolf dressed in sheep's clothing!"

"Where have I heard that from before?" I pissed her off this time.

"Doesn't matter where you heard it from all that matters is that you tricked me. I trusted in you, Paul, and you betrayed my trust. This conversation is done. I need you to leave before you try to hit on our son.

A huge part of me just wanted to go over there and pimp slap her. That was such a low blow, and in front of my kid. But to restrain myself, I immediately thought about Jesse, and I thought about the fact that my father did not raise me to batter women. No matter how bad my mom frustrated him, he never ever laid a hand on her.

I just can't believe my baby mama would fix her mouth to say such a foul thing about me and my son. Me? Hit on my own son? She is definitely losing her marbles, one marble at a time. Not only is it stupid to say that in front of Eliphalet, but now she's going to have my five year old boy thinking that for real. I hope she didn't brainwash my only child. I love that boy, and he's a part of the reason for my change to normalcy.

Why does death have to feel this way? It's already hard to live. But death? Oh, death is a supernatural psychological thriller. It's sort of like the teaser trailer before a movie. I mean, what I am trying to say is, everybody knows what the denotative definition of death is, but until anyone actually gets the ticket from the Grim Reaper when he visits, well, then that's when dying becomes the movie. I'm actually not afraid of dying—anymore--because I realize at this chapter in my life that everyone is dying. I am just a little afraid of death, however. I don't know why? I mean, there's really no reason for me to be afraid because it's going to happen anyway. Right? Only if I had chosen a different path to walk, only if I had chosen to listen to God's voice sooner, I could have done a lot of things differently, but I can't change the one thing that's killing me now. Death. Muerte. It even sounds frightening in Spanish.

Do I deserve to die? Heck yeah! I will not ever pretend like I deserve to live. Jesus died for all the sins of humankind, and as I've learned, there is no sin greater than the other. With the exception of blasphemy or cursing God and...suicide. Committing something like that, acts such as those are unforgiveable.

Do I deserve to live? No, no one deserves to live. We were buried in sin the day that we were born. We learned to lie, cheat and steal before we even entered kindergarten. I know; I was a little devil myself back in the day. But besides all else, besides all things, there's nothing that makes me feel as bad as dying a lonely death. Every day it feels like a knife grows sharper and sharper, pierces deeper and deeper through my heart. At times, I can even feel the pinch, the sting. It feels like freshly squeezed lemon juice being poured over cuts of a thousand razors. Just a little hi or bye from somebody brings great joy to me. I remember Jesse use to call me like every Sunday just to see if I was ok from a night of boos and usually love making. He made me sick when he called me at eight in the morning knowing that I was not up that early. Sometimes I answered, many times I didn't, but I did love the sweet messages he left on my phone.

As I lie here under the covers, crying and crying out for forgiveness and a healing, I wonder, I just wonder who's going to love me?

To

As apart of my last willing testament, I have decided to write a letter to my folks. I'm going to tell my mom and dad the truth about me and this disease of H.I.V. It's time for them to learn everything that's been happening with me since college. Again. No more hiding, no more sheets. No more lies. It's time they know everything about me. But how am I to start this letter?

The last time I spoke to my parents it had to be about a month a go, my mother was in the backyard gardening at the time and my father was watching a movie on television. My father never liked for anyone to disturb him from watching his movie, but he told me that when he saw my number pop up on the Caller I.D. he was filled with glee and hustled to the back where my mother was gardening, he put me on the speakerphone to share a few words of wisdom, laughs and information about my new occupation, never once did I tell them about the disease or Jesse. They know about my son and the issues he was born with but other than that, life has pretty much been hidden from them, I always hated when people gossiped and I knew it wouldn't be long till my parents broke the news to someone other than themselves.

Now it's time for me to break the news, thoughts of confusion bounce in my mind like basketballs, the fear of telling them seems greater than the reward for not telling them. I was never a scholar in school when it came down to writing, so I hope I can write something to them that would not only grasp their attention, but also force them to see the position that I've been placed in as a man trying to find his way.

Dear mom and dad, I write on a piece of crisp, white, college ruled notebook paper. No, no, that's too lame. Too formal. I erase the four words.

Tapping the end of my stencil against my cheek, something else comes to me. It's been about five minutes now. I'll never get this done. Ok. Here I go....

Dear mama and papa, I erase these words, too. They sound too corny. Ok wait a minute. How about I just take the salutation part out and write the darn letter already.

To my parents Will and Alicia Stringer. I honestly can't remember the last time I wrote a letter to you two, but you know what? It doesn't matter because this has to be done. The last couple of years of my life have been crazy. Well, most of my life has been crazy. Ever since the incident with dad's brother, my life ain't ever been the same. It's amazing how slow the time passes when you feel like you about to die. At least that's the way I feel. Tell my siblings I said hello, be careful, and to always use protection. Oops, I shouldn't have said that.

Seriously, seriously I've been diagnosed with H.I.V. My friend Jesse died a couple of weeks because he had AIDS, which succeeds H.I.V. and I just thought that I'd fill you two in on this disease. My doctor got me on all kinds of medications, and from his opinion, I still got a couple of years of good living to achieve my goals. But I'm afraid. I'm very afraid, mom, dad; I'm scared for my life. I don't want to die, at least not this way. Every time I think about this disease, I think about Jesse. Jesse is the guy I was with since I moved away for college. If you didn't know, well you know now. I was living the double life. Sleeping with a woman in the day and chillin' with dudes at night. Believe me, this is absolutely not something I'm proud of, but I just have to tell you this before it's too late.

I miss you two, you know. I miss you two a lot. I'm sorry if I am making you look bad in anyway, but I must say that I'm working on a change with God in my life. Every day it seemed as if I lived my life for a man, but now it's time for me to live my life for a change!

Please don't judge me; just love me like you love my brothers and sisters. By the way, Eliphalet is doing well. He had a successful surgery and that boy is getting big. My baby mama and I haven't been getting along very well, but besides that Eliphalet is straight. I love that boy, and I don't want anything to happen to him like it happened to me.

I want my son to grow up loving women; I don't want him to be like me. I definitely don't want him to be like me. I am so sorry mom and dad. I am so sorry. It's just been so tough for me since I found out I have this murdering disease that's killing me softly. The pastor at the church I started attending talks about faith and miracles a lot. The pastor said that if Jesus could turn water into wine, then he could turn my weakened blood cells into good and normal, healthy blood cells.

All I have besides the thought of you two is faith right now. Otherwise, I feel like my life is already in the grave, and I started digging years ago.

I've been digging and digging up past thoughts, past faults and past things that continue to hurt me to my ivory bones. I know that my choices have not been great, but will you continue to love me? Will you continue to love the boy you birthed into the world all the way back in 1984 and raised to be a man, in spite of his girlish ways? Will you continue to share with me your secrets? I'm not asking for you two to accept that homosexual lifestyle that I once lived, but I am asking you to accept me, your son, not his lifestyle. I still have a few kinks to straighten out. Don't we all? Aren't we all a work in progress?

But what I'm trying to say, Will and Alicia Stringer (mom and dad), is that I love you. And all I want is for you two to love me back the same, no matter what I was or what I've done. You two say that you believe in God, and I'm begging you to please believe in me. I can change; I know it. I can be delivered of this sin and this disease. I know it.

Love,

*Paul Stringer.
P.S. Please pray for me.*

Be

The smell of dandelions, dewberry and iris flowers were not enough to brighten my day on this spring morning. How beautiful they are basking in the sun, saying their sweet *good mornings* and *hello's* to the bees who ask to be their friends. Laying here across the crumpled sheets and warm pillow looking out the window, it's amazing to see how hard these flowers work to stay alive, if all but for a season. They give their very best for God's pleasure, but me, I just can't seem to act right. I guess you can learn a lot about a flower, their relationship with the bee is probably one of the most precious miracles in life. Speaking of a miracle, that's what I need the most, maybe it starts with a flower, or maybe it just starts with me.

What I am is what I be, and yes I know that's not proper English, but that's just how I feel right now. I feel a massive overflow of good things to come, yet at this very state in my life, I feel so bad, so bored, so evil.

What am I to be when people look at me? They see a normal person, but on the inside I'm a freak. I can't do this goody good thing for long. As a matter of fact, I'm tired of playing the record. When will people love me? When will people understand that I'm sorry for my wrongs, but I sure can't take them back now? When will people look at me like they look at the spring flowers and just enjoy my company? I am a human that thrives off of love, not a foreign mammal created in some university science lab as an experiment.

I mailed off a letter to my parents two weeks ago and still haven't heard anything from them yet. Even they don't love me anymore. My heart skipped a beat, maybe two beats or even three. But what's there to love in me? My life has been washed up, wasted, done, zero! "I hate me! I hate me!" I unconsciously hit the bed causing one of my pillows to sling to the side. I'm beginning to lose it.

Let me call up the church, see if the pastor is there.

Ring, the phone went for a few seconds, my grip on this cellular device is even stronger, waiting for someone to answer.

One thing about a church phone, it loves to ring at least twenty times before someone picks up. Ring and ring it goes until finally someone says, "Hello? This is the desk of the church. How may I help you?" The secretary whispers over the phone. Her voice sounds sexy enough to get a saved brother unsaved, but she also gets on my nerves.

"Yes, I would like to speak with the pastor," I modestly speak, but really I was anxious to speak with the pastor.

"Well, the pastor is very busy, may I take a message." It seems like that's her programmed message every time I call. The pastor is always busy according to her. She might as well forward calls to his voicemail.

"No, I'm good. I'll just," a voice in the background interjects.

"Who's that on the phone?" an overflowing, rich and stern voice embraces the mouth piece of the phone on the opposite end of my line.

"Some young man is on the phone to speak to you, Pastor," the secretary whimpers. I listen attentively to their discourse.

"Well, did you get his name?" Sounds like the pastor's voice.

"No, he said he'll call back later," the secretary speaks, awkwardly, with fear and reverence in her voice.

With a strong authority, I hear the pastor say, "Let me hold the phone." Static from the hasty exchange of the receiver from one speaker to the other fills the dead air.

"Hello young man. To who am I speaking with?" He pauses, waiting for my response.

"This is Paul," I murmur like a shy Boy Scout asking for Girl Scout cookies.

"Hey Paul, how are you doing my buddy?" Before I give a reply, he warmly asks, "what's going on son?"

"Well sir, I've been going through some severe episodes of depression and I just felt like I needed to speak with you."

"Ok, ok. Come on over to the church in about thirty minutes. We can talk. I need to pick up some lunch, first. And then--we'll talk." I imagine the pastor still wearing his mourning clothes: dark fedora, dark glasses resting on his nose, heavy dark cloak buttoned to his throat, black slacks, and black dress shoes. His voice, though, didn't sound morbid at all. Actually, it sounded like sunshine, if sunshine could ever make a sound. Needless to say, his sunshiny voice brightened my day.

"Hey son, know this. With God everything is going to be alright. You have power over that depression. You hear me Paul, you hear me?" I can hear the change in his countenance: furrowed brows, glaring teeth. I know he means what he says. He believes what he says. He hates any form of doubt or fear, for God has not given us the spirit of fear. Fear, fake evidence appearing real, was a trick of the devil. And Pastor...well, he had a vendetta against Satan.

"Yes sir," I concur with conviction, feeling the wounds which seem to not heal.

"I'll see you in thirty minutes then," we both hang up at once.

I jump up from my sorrowful position: face down in the bed, head smothered in a pillow, sheets held tightly, covering my weeping face. I dash into the bathroom and take a quick cold shower. I have to rinse the stench of feeling sorry from myself from my body. Otherwise, I am afraid the pastor might observe how bad of shape I'm really in. I step out while the water is still running, twist the knob, and reach for my towel. It reeks. I definitely need to end this everlasting pity party I'm relishing and do laundry. I find whatever pair of non-skinny jeans and loose fitting polo shirt that's lying around to pull on.

I stick my feet in some shoes, though not matching, and head for the door. I have twenty minutes to make it to the church. I grab my deodorant and swipe under each arm. After splashing a little cologne on to further eliminate the smell of self-pity, I leave the deodorant and cologne on a table next to the front door as I exit and pull it behind me. I'm so looking forward to talking with Pastor. We can talk, he said. These days, he was about the only person willing to talk to me. I'm grateful.

"Ok son, I'm going to have to ask you straight up. What is it that you want to be?" The pastor immediately begins his interrogation session before I can even get comfortable in my chair.

Lost and confused by what he is asking me, I gave him this response: "What do you mean by that, Pastor?"

"What I mean is that you have to choose one, son. You're either heterosexual or homosexual. There is no in between," he stares at me with monumental sincerity. I can't help but feel that he really cares about my struggles and shortcomings that I've faced throughout the years.

"You know which one I choose pastor," I reply matter-of-factly.

"And what's that?" he rises a little in his seat as if he is waiting for me to give my Grammy winning answer.

Oh, he's really going to make me say it. It's not like I haven't told him before.

"Heterosexual, sir. I choose to be heterosexual. I, Paul Stringer, choose to be straight and the good Lord is my witness." I sound redundant, but I needed Pastor to believe me; I needed to believe me. So who was I trying to convince here?

"So what's the problem, then, young man?" he inquires.

"I don't know. It's hard. The other lifestyle is constantly beating across my chest like a rubber bullet, piercing and tough on impact, and then bouncing back off." I am agitated right now; I really hate talking about this at times. I know, though, that talking about it, accepting my past life in all its grandeur as well as its expiry is all a part of the healing process. Time heals all.

"You know what that is son? God has his shield of protection around you. Whenever you get those thoughts, you need to rebuke those negative perverted thoughts in the name of Jesus Christ! Son, let me tell you something. It sounds to me like you're going through symptoms of withdrawal, and that's okay. We all go through this phase with any vice. Don't think that your past sins are greater than another, and they certainly aren't greater than God." He's sitting across from me in a matching arm chair, signifying that he's on my level. No, not gay, but seen as my equal in the eyes of God. God has no respect of persons, I know. His slouched posture was inviting, comforting altogether. At this very moment he seems down to earth, unreal, nothing like what he seems to be at services. He's wearing denim. A white collared shirt with his name, position, and the church logo stitched on the left breast pocket. A handkerchief is stuffed in it. His shirt is starched and ironed to a crisp, but it's not buttoned to his throat. His cuffs are not buttoned either. I see his feet are dressed in thick, white, cotton socks and black dress shoes.

"The only evidence from your past sins that has caught up to you is the H.I.V., and I'm sure that's the main thing that's been depressing you." He makes so much sense. I wish other pastors were like him, not quick to judgment, but relentless to talk and show that they have a general concern for my issues, not my wallet. Heck, I wish more people in general were as down to earth and welcoming as he is.

"Yes it has. I feel like a big dummy." Maybe, I ponder, I am a big dummy.

"Stop beating yourself up so badly," he looks away from me and whispers a quick prayer that only he and the Lord God are privy to .

"I know, I know, but my moms and dad haven't even replied back to the letter I sent them. I poured out my heart, but they didn't even acknowledge that they received the letter. It's been two weeks since I mailed that letter. Depression was beginning to resurface within me.

"Hey brother," the pastor interrupts my pity party once more, "there is no need for heartache and pain. Cast your cares upon the Lord and he shall renew your strength. Remember this brother, no matter what you've done; your parents will always love you. You just have to give them time to get around to it, because this is certainly new news for them. I know that our daddy in heaven will always love you, son; like Joshua, he knew you before you were even thought of, even conceived in the womb."

"Wow," he shifts in his seat to face me more directly, "look at how handsome you are. You can have plenty of women speaking gibberish at the sight of you. Their words would stumble over their tongue if they tried to speak to you," he smiles. I know this is all a part of the healing process, too. It was working. He was boosting my self-esteem. I had hope that I would be able to love again. Perhaps I would meet the woman of my dreams.

"Don't ever doubt the beauty that God has placed in you both physically and spiritually, Paul." he continues, his smile slightly faded. "You were wonderfully and majestically made for His glory, for His honor, and His praise," he clasps his course hands together with a thump. Pokes his chest and says, "Even when the dark clouds of homosexuality come upon your life, know that He who created the deep blue seas and the stars which stretch through eternity, know that He loves you.

When the disease entered your blood cells, He already knew about it. When the crowds of judgment come knocking on your door, just know that He can handle it. God is so awesome and worthy to be praised!" he lifts both hands in the air, extending all phalanges on each hand, as if giving God two high-fives. "Do you believe that?" he returns to his previous position and tilts his head toward me, reading me with his eyes.

"Yes sir," I say, drenched with tears of joy, wet all over my shirt, filled with the washing of the Holy Spirit all over my life. Never have I felt such a peace about myself before, a peace that indeed passes beyond all understanding.

"How do you feel son?" He smiles at me.

"I feel better than good sir. I feel awesome! I feel relieved, and I feel the power of God all over my body. I feel like much has been accomplished in this short time of talking with you. I glance at the clock. I've been sitting in this seat for an hour already. Time flies when you're praising God.

"And I know that I have to give my parents some time to come around," I conclude.

"Son, let me tell you something, Nothing good ever comes easy in life. But all things work together for the good of them that love God the Father and Jesus Christ the Son of God.

We must all wake up out of our ungodly sleep and know to do what's right before the sight of the Lord. See son, it doesn't matter how you messed up or how many times you've messed up. What matters my brother," he slaps both hands on his knees, "is that God through Jesus Christ will deliver you from all sins and shame." He stands up from his seat. "He will keep you cherished in the right mind and work an extraordinary deliverance in your life, the type of deliverance that he's doing for you now." He pauses, gives me another stern look. I guess he is reading me again, seeing if I take heed his words. Then, with one giant step, he's nearly positioned in front of me.

"Do you believe that son?" He grasps my hands, and pulls me up to his level.

Standing, I say, "Yes sir," at an even greater level of attention.

"Well, let's seek God in our closing prayer."

Straight

Waking up this morning, I had to swallow a small pill called pride. Yes I'm guilty! I'm very guilty of it. How strange that it would be to feel and see the beauty of a new day looking at me. I mean, just yesterday it felt like the turbines of a plane were twisting toward me. I felt really down, depressed, and somewhat down the drain. But through it all, God has blessed me to see another day. How wonderful and awesome it feels to know about a God who loves me in spite of my past. When everyone else is ready to nail me to the cross, God says no. God says that the cross has already been taken by His son, Jesus Christ.

Honestly, I don't know, I really don't know what my future has in store for me. But I know one thing, even if this disease over takes me, even if H.I.V. brings me down to my knees, I can still say amen, God is good. Amen, God is good!

On that note, it would be wise of me to take a shower and get some grub, maybe I'll cook breakfast, a little bit of smooth cheese grits and eggs over well will take no time at all. Ahhh... the thought of hot grits and eggs, maybe I should spice it up with some crispy pork bacon and orange juice with a lot of pulp. I would even love to have a freshly baked steam simmering from off the top with honey doing a dance in between a biscuit. Wait a minute, I don't have all of that, I may just need to go to *Stella's* down the street for a good hearty meal. It's Saturday, I have all day to do whatever I want, no job to answer to, and hopefully no baby mama to annoy me. I will declare this day as just a day to spend with my God.

  Arriving back home from Stella's and *full* is certainly not the appropriate word to describe how blessed my stomach feel. I feel like I just ate a pig, but that certainly was not what I ordered, with the exception of the bacon crackling in my mouth as it made its way down to King Stomach. The waiters are always very nice and the people there have never been quick to judge, everybody always seems to be so friendly there, even the regular customers that patronize the restaurant. It has that smooth jazz type of feel when you walk in with history making African-American figures posted all throughout the restaurant. Martin Luther King Jr. is the centerpiece and other greats such as President Barack Obama, Michael Jordan, Langston Hughes, Mary McLeod Bethune, Oprah and Tyler Perry dot each part of the restaurant with a synopsis under their picture mentioning what each one of them have contributed to the world. The only picture that's missing is a picture of Jesus, but then again the bible does speak about not having any graven images of Him.

Stella's is not short of religion though, on each table there is a different scripture, when I first began eating there, I tried to find a different table every time, just to see what scripture was placed on that particular table. That was my little inspiration on days when I was in college and had nothing to be inspired by.

Besides the cheese grits, eggs, bacon, biscuits and orange juice I had today, their menu has many selections and their prices are very feasible, my meal only cost me five bucks and the orange juice was just a dollar extra. Stella's is located just a block west of Francis State University. Believe it or not, although Stella's is right by the college, mostly the old heads are the one's eating there. With the exception of their college nights on Thursday's, the crowd is usually thirty-five and older.

I have an incoming call. I wonder who this could be. No one ever calls me this early on a Saturday. Hopefully it's not a bill collector; all my bills should be up to date. Oh, but wait, I do have that student loan that I'm two months behind on, maybe that's who's calling, *the loan company*. I'll just give them some sort of excuse to get them off the phone. Where the heck is my phone? It stopped ringing.

It's ringing again. There it is, right on the kitchen counter where I left it. Oh, I can't believe who this is, can't be, not in a million years. Feeling anxious and not knowing what to say or how to say it, I freeze. I totally freeze as I watch the phone continue to ring as I saw her name lit bright on the Caller I.D.

"Hello son, this is your mother." Wow, it can't be. I know this is not my mom on the line. Immediately, I weep. Tears flow from my eyes like the Niagara Falls. I feel weird.

"Mother, what's going on? I haven't heard from you in a while."

"Son, I received your letter you sent to your father and me. I couldn't help but to fall down on my knees and pray for you after what I read. I've been crying," she coughs to hold back yet another weeping spell, "at least twice a day ever since I heard the news. My heart has been heavy, your father is a little disappointed, but I just want you to know, Paul that we love you in spite of. With that letter, that letter brought me the closest to you; I felt your heart and your spirit in that letter. I felt the little Paul I knew way before your uncle took advantage of you. I felt my little boy again. Paul, I felt my little boy needing help and I as your mother must come to help you."

Her tears brought back memories, memories of the demons which tried to destroy me when I was only a little boy, oh how she cries a familiar cry. A cry of anger and a cry f grace, now look at us over twenty year's later feeling like we are in that same familiar place. Her face glowed through the darkness of my situation and she cried and prayed for me like no one else could. That day when she found out I was molested I didn't just recognize the love of a mother, but I now understand that the love from my creator was also in that room. Oh how I miss my mother, it's been a little while since I've seen her and pops, actually I think the last time I saw them was at my collegiate graduation, and that had to be at least two years ago.

The pain I saw in her eyes and the fragileness I recognized when I last saw her was surely not the strong, silky black hair, vibrant skin and funny woman I grew to know as a child, no, she was a lot different when I last saw her. I could still see the pain in her eyes and hear the fear in her voice. After grandma had died, a lot had changed with our family, so much till I don't know where to begin.

"Paul, are you still there." My mother woke me out of my trance.

"Yes mom, I'm still here." I looked around the room with a smile.

" I'm sorry I wasn't there before. I'm sorry I haven't been there, but I will be there this time. I will be there for you from here on out. I want to see you, Paul. I want to see you so badly, my son. Your father and I are planning a trip to drive from South Florida on up to Tallahassee. As a matter of fact, son, we will be on our way up their tomorrow.

First and foremost son, I just ask for your forgiveness for all that we have done wrong to you, including doubting you, not giving you an ear to hear or a shoulder to cry on. I just am so sorry for what happened between you and your uncle and whatever else went wrong during your childhood. I, I ..." her words are tangled with her weeping. I can hardly make anything else out.

"Mom, it's okay. I accept your plea for forgiveness. I am just so happy to speak with you. You know going through this whole ordeal has had me thinking about a lot of things. Of course you and dad and my siblings have been on the top of my list, as well as my son.

I've thought very seriously on the subject of death, and you know what? I can't control the destiny which God has planned for me. If he sees fit for me to die in the next few years or maybe even in the next few months, that's fine with me because death is at the end of all of our destinies.

Unless Jesus comes back today, all of us living now will have the period at the end of a pastor's speech. And I realized that more than ever when I attended Jesse's funeral."

"Jesse was the young man that gave you the disease?" I can hear the concern, a little hate toward Jesse, in her voice.

"I don't really know, ma. It could have been someone else."

"Well, how is your son?" She quickly changes the subject.

"He's doing okay." I automatically reply. I guess he's doing okay. Truth is, I haven't seen him or heard from Kim in weeks.

"That's good," my mother speaks softer now, the joy of her hearing my voice seems to have left her.

"So you and dad are really coming up tomorrow? I'm totally shocked," I announce. "But," emphatic pause, "I'm terribly happy that you all are coming. Your visit gives me an excuse for cleaning my house, getting back in order."

"Yes son, we will be there to see you, love you and support you. Besides, it's about time we take a trip to the great capital of Florida."

"How long will you two be here?" I'm not sure if I really want the answer to that, but I guess I got to know. I have to be prepared.

"We will be there for as long as it takes. Goodbye son, I love you more than you could ever imagine."

"Good bye mom, I love you too and look forward to seeing you soon." We both hang up, feeling as if we have reached a common goal. At least I feel like I have accomplished what needed to be accomplished. A phone call from my mom.

"Wow my son, look at you. My son. You look really different. And you look like you've lost some weight. Come give your mother a hug. We didn't come all the way from Miami to not love you." My mother looks gorgeous, with her full head of jet black hair, eyes sparkling and a trimmed up weight, she looks like the model I knew once when I was a child. Unlike the last time I saw her, she is full of strength and as they say *black don't crack*, not a wrinkle dots her face. I am absolutely stunned at this figure standing before me.

As she swallows me in her bosom, I just want to cry. Lord, I just want to cry. I seriously can't believe this. I can't believe this right here is happening. Here comes my dad. My father is pretty built himself, although he'd never been the gym type of guy, he's always had the biceps of a football player and the legs of a track runner.

"Son, no matter what you do or what you are, your mom and I will still love you. And we will support you one-hundred percent. Come give your father a hug. I love you my son. You were my first born. That means you are just that much more special to me." I hope so, I think inwardly.

"Mom says that you two will be here for as long as it takes," I state, releasing my father from our lingering embrace.

"Your mom was right by saying that," my father laughs it off.

"Good, because I have to go see the doctor tomorrow and see what he has to say about me."

"Is this the doctor that told you that you were infected with H.I.V." My mother's eyes tilted up, as if she just said the one comment that brought the elephant in the building.

"Yes." I simply respond, no need to get frustrated over spoiled milk.

"Well with God, I'm sure it's going to be good news," my mom chimes.

"I hope so," I look at the both of them."

"So, are you going to let us in your home, you don't have any roommates, right?"

"Right, come on in and put your bags to the left. Are you hungry?

"Starving," they chorus.

"Would you two like to eat here or go out to dinner?"

"We can go out. I'll let Alicia get freshened up while I catch a game or something on ESPN. You okay with that baby?" my father asks mom. My father is also making himself comfortable. He found a good spot in the living area in front of the T.V., leaving mom to do all the unpacking.

"You the man, Will. Always will be." I can't tell if mom is actually okay with it or being sarcastic. "It sounds good to me," she turns to face me. "How about you Paul?"

"It sounds good to me, too. I'm tired of cooking noodles and chicken," I gesture my head toward my semi-clean kitchen. "Maybe we can go to a seafood place or something."

"Sounds good. I'll go freshen up a bit and take a power nap. I should be ready to go in about an hour." She heads to the nearest bed, which happens to be in my room. I'm glad I changed the linen first thing this morning when I peeled myself out of bed. "Don't let your dad take a power nap, because if he does, he'll never wake up." She winks at me and disappears into my room.

"Now this is pretty nice Paul. Nice music playing in the background and the crabs are excellent."

"Thought you'd like it here, mom. How about you dad? Are you enjoying the catfish and cheese grits?"

"Yes son it's delicious. Tastes like the way grandma used to make it. I'm impressed. How is your food?"

"Good, good," I describe with grits dripping from my lips.

"So Paul, tell us a little about this disease."

"Well, as you two already know, I am H.I.V. positive," I begin, thinking this isn't exactly dinner table conversation. But since moms asked, I'll be obedient and answer. "I contracted the disease from sleeping with a guy. I have a really good feeling that it was my friend..." I clear my throat for correction, "my boyfriend, Jesse, who recently died of A.I.D.S." I divert my eyes to the yellow cheese grits that are spreading like molasses, overtaking my plate. I do not want to look into their eyes, judgmental, disapproving. I feel an unwelcoming but familiar feeling creeping up on me. It's depression.

"Even before I found out about my friend Jesse dying of A.I.D.S., God started working on my own heart with this homosexuality thing," I continue, finding the courage to lift my head. After all, God promised to be strong when I am weak. And this feels like one of the weakest moments of my life. Verbally explaining this to my parents, over a plate of seafood and grits, is more weakening than the moment the doctor revealed to me my imminent demise. "And as of a few weeks ago, I must confess that I am completely straight." My dad looks like he's about to interrupt. But I'm relieved to not see hate, judgment, or bitterness in his facial expression.

"So what does that mean son?" He partially looks up at me.

"What it means is the fact that I have no desire whatsoever to be with a man," I proclaim. "Zero, zilch, nothing. My desire is the way it's supposed to be, naturally. And that desire is to have the love of a woman on my heart."

"Amen, amen," my mother professes.

"I'm so happy that God has set me free from those demons that constantly troubled my soul," I continue. There is no stopping me now.

The thing about God is that he can work a change in us to be what he wants us to be. No homosexuality has any power over me in the name of Jesus Christ!"

"Wow son I felt that conviction. I felt that, Paul."

"Yes, the Lord delivered me from that lifestyle, and as you know the word says whomever the son sets free is truly free indeed."

"So, tomorrow? What is the doctor's appointment about?"

"Well, I took another test for H.I.V., per my doctor's request. I took one six months after my initial diagnosis. I took another three months after that. Of course the last two were positive, but I'm trying to see if anything has changed this time." I am certainly hoping and believing so. It's been a total of twelve months since my initial diagnosis.

"That's right son. You keep the good faith. Miracles do happen. You will be healed of the disease in the name of Jesus Christ!" My mom yells across the table, bringing attention to our heated conversation.

"Sorry about that people, you can get back to eating," my dad interrupts and says," well son, we support you. And I am extremely happy that God is working on your heart like that."

"Yes God has, and He still is."

"Are you ready to go mom and dad?"

"Yeah we're ready, my mom and dad said together."

"Lets go!"

"Check please," Father requests. "Oh and also three to-go boxes will also due. Honey, we will finish this food and conversation at Paul's apartment, don't need folks round this fine establishment knowing our business.

"Yep, the people are really friendly here, but they will know every last details of your business if you talk about it at *Stella's*." The waitress delivered the bill with our to-go boxes, then we quietly exited the restaurant.

A cool breeze followed us out of the restaurant; all three of us turned around and quickly dismissed it.

"Okay Mr. Stringer, you can come on back now," My doctor waves for me. The same nervousness and chills I felt the first time coming here, seems to have come back with a vengeance. My heart is fluttering, oh no! I'm having a panic attack; I can't stand to be in the presence of this doctor right now, *the bearer of bad news*. I ask if my parents are welcomed in the back with me. Maybe they will be the source of comfort, I so deeply desire.

"Of course parental support is good, especially for you, you're going to need it." That doesn't sound so good. I hope the good doctor has better news once we get inside the infamous back room.

"Okay Mr. Stringer, we decided to do an overall S.T.D. test to see what else you may have contracted, unknowingly. I'm afraid the news is not good." Well, if this was the case, I really didn't want to hear it.

"Okay, Doctor Mark, go ahead. Don't beat around the bush."

"In no particular order, we tested you for gonorrhea, and you tested negative for that. Syphilis is negative, crabs is negative, and herpes Mr. Stringer," he looks up at me, I knew that it was the warning bells for the bad news he was about to deliver. I took a deep breath as I watched him spit out, "herpes Mr. Stringer is positive," he looks up from his chart. "Yes I know it must pain you to hear that. I'm sorry."

Now, as for H.IV., you understand this is your third test? The odds of having a change in report are perhaps, eh, a million to one," he guesses. I can almost hear the sarcasm in his voice. Nevertheless, I'm sitting on the edge of my seat, trying to suppress the doubt and depression I feel crawling inside me, ready to surface at any given moment. I'm starting to feel unstable. The last impromptu counseling session I had with Pastor comes to mind. I can hear his reassurance ringing in my ears. I pray his unmovable, unshakable faith that I will be healed, cured of this illness, activates within me. Activate your faith, I command myself. I glance over the faces of my parents. My eyes rest in the eyes of my mother.

I remember the talk I had with Jesse's mom the day of his funeral. She was so sincere, so encouraging, refreshing even. I was overjoyed to learn that Jesse would get to spend eternity in heaven. Still sitting on the edge, I grip my seat as tight as a fisherman grips his reel when he's caught a big one. But the urge to give in to reality won. I decide that whether the report is good or bad, I will still walk away with my head held high, knowing that I am loved and I am saved. I look into the eyes of both my parents. They return a reassuring gaze. I smile at mother first. She touches her heart and then gestures her hand as if releasing her heart, her love to me. There's nothing like a woman's love, a mother's love. Then, I smile at my father. He nods, pounds his fist against his chest, and stands as boldly as Tarzan. I do the same. I suck in my gut and stick out my chest. My eyes are dead center with the glassy eyes of the doctor in the white trench coat. I'm ready for my verdict.

His eyes hold me in their stare when he says, "You tested negative."

"What?" I question, not able to believe what I just heard.

The doctor begins to speak again, "Yes, you heard me correctly. You tested negative for H.I.V."

"I---I just don't know how to respond to that." I slump in my chair. Mom and Dad are at either side of me, showering me in their kisses and hugs. I feel a little smothered. I know I heard the doctor diagnose me with herpes, but living with herpes seems like a hurdle to jump over, while living with AIDS seemed like it was an unmovable mountain. Goodbye to taking eight pills, some twice a day, others three times a day. Goodbye barely-there social life. Hello love of my life.

"I really don't know either," the doctor interrupts our family bonding moment, "because twice you tested positive. You are a medical miracle," he winks. "Miracles happen every day son. Many times we just don't give God the time to manifest them in the natural. "

I'm crying, my mom is crying, and I'm just flabbergasted. Is this doctor for real? Or is he some kind of undercover angel on assignment?

"Praise God! Praise God!" My father is singing, lifting his arms on high, and he is right indeed. Praise be to God. The doctor leaves the room, allowing us to rejoice in this day the Lord has made.

We arrive back to my apartment feeling like we all just slayed a giant, God gave me the rock and the sling shot, while my faith took the rock the distance it needed for me to be healed. No longer does that giant of H.I.V. have any power or authority over me, because now, right now it's dead and I'm free.

Through the battles with depression, through the hurt and the pain, this is a prime example to let people know that God still is in control. God is good. He is so awesome and He sits on the throne. I'm just so overwhelmed by his grace, mercies and passion for me. A lot of times we just expect God to do things because he's God, but we have to remember that God is not our own personal secretary. He surely will not do what is not in his will to do, so I thank him for this supernatural healing. He healed me from H.I.V. and delivered me out of homosexuality. What else can I ask for from a God like this, a God who's in control of everything?

"Paul, are you okay?" My mother looks at me sideways.

"Yes, yeah, I'm just meditating on how blessed I am. How God has done this miraculous thing for me. I-- I just don't know what to do with myself."

My mother laughs, "Paul, baby, realize that you never gave up on life. You could have easily committed suicide or did some kind of craziness to yourself. But you didn't son; you didn't. Through the storm, you decided to live and let God. Of course we've never condoned homosexuality, but we could have at least looked at the situation from your point of view. We don't exactly know how hard it was for you dealing with your uncle at such a young age, we can only assume. Whatever the assumption, we constantly tried to brush your being molested off as if it didn't happen. You are twenty-six years old now and you have a son to raise and protect.

I am so happy that my boy Eli will grow up to see the better me, Oh my gosh I have to tell my pastor the good news, and I wonder what Jesse's mom would think once she finds out that I'm not only straight, but H.I.V. free, so many people to call, so many words to say.

My mother snaps me back into her world. Her face shines bright as the evening sun resting on the mountainous peeks of Colorado. My father is behind her, this time he is the cheerleader and mother is the quarterback. She's giving me all the plays and he's cheering me on, I guess it's great to be on a winning team, the bible says where two or more are gathered together in His name, so is He. I sincerely believe that Jesus is right here, our coach, our commander in chief, giving my mother all the plays to give to me.

"You must show your son what it is to be a man, a man who God has called you to be, Paul. In your younger days, we didn't quite go to church like we should have, but God has placed us in some humbling situations which caused us to seek him. So son, we love you, we just want the best for you.

Right now is your awakening, your path to newness. Allow the Lord to lead your life on a path to happiness and feel free to share your testimony on what God has done for your life. Jesus died so you may have life; Jesse died so that you may have strength. So, what will you die for?"

"Mom, I've already died; I've died a battle to be straight. And straight I am through the love of Christ Jesus. Straight I shall proclaim and straight I will be forever until the day when God calls my name."

Epilogue: The Professor

*C*an anyone tell me the meaning of life? Science holds the foundational elements to discovering who we are and what we are as human beings. Without the study of science we have no knowledge of our atmosphere, we certainly wouldn't understand the basic human genome principals, and without science many of you would not even bear to recognize that the air we breathe is a liquid, not a solid."

The classroom is silent, a pen drop would be loud at this moment, everyone is in awe of the professor, quenching every move he makes and mimicking on their papers every word he spews out.

The Professor continues, "Many individuals like to wrap up science into one bundle and expect for everything to make sense. Can any one explain to me the very definition of science?" He eyes one of the students raising his hand in the back.

"Yes. Go ahead, Chris, in the back there."

"Uh… Sir… Science is like the systematic enterprise," he had looked up the definition on Wikipedia from his Smartphone. He is looking down at his phone and informing the professor of what he was supposed to have read in class the week prior. "Science builds and organizes knowledge in the form of testable explanations and predictions about the universe." Chris lets out a gasp of air, then sits back down in the corner of the classroom, a place he loves best, to be alone.

"Thank you young man. You receive an *A* for regurgitation." Although the young man was clearly reading from his phone, he still missed a few pointers.

" Science, ladies and gentlemen, as you turn in your textbooks to page thirty-two," the crackling of pages broke the silence of the students as some pulled out the hardcover textbook, while others just opened the application on their electronic reading device. "Science is the phenomena of the material universe and their laws, sometimes with implied exclusions of pure mathematics." He paused for a few seconds from his lecture and wrote a few of the notes on his white board.

Science has captivated the minds of such greats as Kepler, Galileo and of course Newton, but today, ladies and gentleman, I want to tell you about a different kind of science. Now I know that this is not a religious study class; this is a basic Collegiate Science class, so those of you who may feel uncomfortable about the One who invented science, then you have a free pass for today. But for those of you who would like to stay, I promise you, you are in for a treat."

A few of the students dressed in black Goth clothing with trench coats and trinkets, and some of the hip-hop heads with skulls and bones advertised across their shirts leave the room. Altogether, approximately fifteen students leave, leaving twenty-five more hunched over their seats drooling for what the professor has to deliver.

"You see class science as we know it would not have been made possible without the One who healed the sick. Some call it science; I call it a miracle. The One who raised the dead, some call it science; I call it a miracle. The One who fed thousands with just a few fish and bread. Some even call that science. I call it a miracle. Many people believe that this Earth was formed with a big bang, and I as a teacher am required to teach you that. I assure you I will teach you about the big bang theory, but before anybody can fix their mouths to say big bang theory, I'm going to tell you about my Big-God, He is not just based upon some scientific theory, He is real! "

The seriousness of the words he spoke were expressed on his face, the conviction the professor felt crossed over the podium and had each student's full attention.

"And it is simple as this: For God so loved the world that he gave His only begotten Son, that who-so-ever shall believe in Him shall prosper and have eternal life."

Many of the students look around, some speechless, some blow the professor off. Eighteen more students leave the room. Now it is down to seven. Some leave murmuring under their breaths, some leave as quiet as a snake roaming through the garden. Regardless of how they left, they all turned their backs on the professor and the message he is conveying.

"To those of you who have decided to stay, this message is for you. Science told me that I would not be healed of the disease called H.I.V. Many of you know of it and probably have had some family members die of the eventual progression to AIDS."

The professor pauses for a few seconds, picks up the tears that fell with a used napkin that was sitting on the podium, surveys the class once more, and then he continues with pure emotion and fervor.

"I am a living testimony that God usurps the world of science. Yes I am a science professor, but the more and more I learn and teach; the more I understand how the science of everything in life eventually goes back to God. The very breath that we breathe, the very songs of deliverance that we sing, each and everything that lives, must die. And in our dying our soul will find a place. For some, that place will be glorious. For others that place will be miserable."

Chris raises his hands again interrupting the professor's speech. "But Professor Stringer, you mean to tell me that we are just taking this class for nothing?" The class erupted in chatter.

"No son, that's not at all what I'm telling you. What I'm telling you is that science is based on hypotheses and theories, all which unless are tested and proven are just that--hypotheses and theories. My doctor prescribed me all the medications in the world, but no medication could give me the overwhelming power of faith in God to heal me of that disease.

It's a reason that it's only seven of you left in this class today. Seven is the number of completion, and on the seventh day God rested. My time here is up; just ask yourselves this question, students. What will it take to make your life complete? I promise you we will tackle every question you ever had about science, but I will present the aforementioned on the basis of faith.

"Professor Stringer, would it be wrong to believe in the big bang theory and be a Christian, too?" Anna uncomfortably asked.

"Well Anna, I'll tell you this--to believe in anything outside of the word of God as a Christian is strictly *Out of Order!*"

A Reading Group Guide:

Dying To Be Straight!

Michael D. Beckford

Paul Stringer faced some spiritual demons; these demons had one mission, a mission to take his life away. But as you have read, what the enemy may try to do for bad, God can turn that around and do it for our good. So, let's see how much you have retained from reading this novella.

This reading guide can be a good source for book clubs, teachers, parents, and those in ministry whom decide to use this book as a tool for deliverance and counseling. May God bless you. Hope you enjoyed.

Discussion Questions

1. Approximately what age range was Paul Stringer when he was sexually molested by his uncle?

2. What relative discovered that Paul Stringer was being molested by his uncle?

3. At what age did Paul Stringer begin to twist like a girl?

4. What would you consider Paul Stringer's defining moment in the fifth grade?

5. Why was Paul Stringer bullied in middle school?

6. What was a defining moment in Paul's sixth grade year that made him feel free of homosexuality?

7. Do you feel that an individual having a relationship with the opposite sex automatically makes them heterosexual?

8. Who is Brian?

9. In the chapter **Hangin Out,** what do you feel Paul Stringer was trying to express with this quote, "**How can we feel both in love and lonely at the same time?**"

10. While Paul Stringer was attending the Hope Christian Private School a mysterious individual approached Paul and revealed a few things about Paul's life? Would you consider that individual to be a Prophet, an Angel, Jesus, or just an ordinary person who knew a few things about Paul?

11. Did Paul Stringer consider Dave to be a lover or a friend?

12. What was Paul and Dave's favorite thing to do in the car, in their high school parking lot?

13. Who did Paul attend the prom with during his junior year of high school?

14. In the beginning of what chapter is this quote taken from, "How can a man be a man, if he does not know why he is a man?"

15. What is the name of Paul Stringer's son, and what does his name mean?

16. Did Paul make the right move by moving in with his girlfriend?

17. What disease did Jesse die of?

18. What's the name of the commercially well known song that was sung at Jesse's funeral?

19. If Paul wasn't molested by his uncle, do you believe that he still would have dealt with the

same struggles of homosexuality throughout his adolescent and young adult life?

20. A close relative of Jesse asked Paul this, "Are you saved young man?" Who was that relative, and why did that individual ask him that question?

21. Paul was diagnosed with H.I.V., was his girlfriend diagnosed with the disease as well?

22. Paul Stringer wanted to take his own life, what individual would you say helped him find reason to keep it?

23. In the last chapter of the book, Paul Stringer told his mother that he had already died, what was he referring to?

24. What dramatic event happened in Paul Stringer's life that made him to declare a change from his homosexual lifestyle?

25. Who was Paul Stringer's greatest enemy throughout the entire book?

Special Sneak Peek of the Sequel to
"Dying To Be Straight!" Dying To Be Straight! Too

Dying To Be Straight Too!

MICHAEL D. BECKFORD

Available *Now* wherever books are sold.

Prologue: Club S

After the first two seconds of meeting a guy, I wish I had never met him. Life on the streets was dirty, but it didn't get dirtier than a pimp. Yes, I said pimp. The very nature of a disgusting thing, which I simply can't imagine dating ever again. So, there it goes, my declaration for the separation of my very existence from the male gender. Yes, I am done with the xy chromosome, and I am happy and deeply satisfied with the double x.

People are out here thinking this is a game. This here ain't no game! This is life, man. This is my life. Time out for wearing skirts, dresses, and tight linens. Now is the time for baggie jeans, slacks, and sometimes balling shorts. I don't have anybody to impress. I impress myself because I gets mine.

My man used to make me out to be his whore on Sunday and a video vixen for the world on Monday. Yeah, that's right. We made movies, too. Some may say that I was just as much of a dog as he was because I did enjoy the sex. Nevertheless, it wasn't about that.

She looked down; scars from relationships past had her mind bouncing faster than the music that was being played in the club. Her heart never seemed to forgive itself. The malice she felt for her ex was as sharp as a double-edged sword.

The dullness in her figure spoke volumes towards her discontent. Normally, when she was in a room full of women. She was barely able to pour ice on her hormones quick enough. But that particular Saturday night at Club Sodom was a little bit different for Alexis Carter.

It wasn't about the sex at all. It was about all the hell he put me through and got away with. He was only a man of his word when it came down to seeing me at night. "That Devil!"

Her faint screams were barely recognizable over the booming music. She posted her tiny hips up against the wall. Then, a small tear formed, and another released like hot chocolate on a cold winter's day. But the only thing that was cold about Alexis was her heart.

One by one, each tear represented a specific hurt. Each tear released a particular weight. But her tears went unnoticed. Her tears were like the backdrop of a stage play, they seemed to have written their lines for the rehearsal to the destruction of her life.

With the deep absence of light in the club, besides being at the bar, no one was able to see a thing. Visions of hatred had formed as her tears continued to release memories of sorrow and pain. She lusted after hate for which she harbored against a man who she believed would never care about her again.

Everything he said was based on broken promises. The dude filled my head up with illusions with his sweet talk and seductive touch. He had me believing that I would live the life of a Hollywood star.

He blew my head up with dreams that my name would be on 'The Walk of Fame' and a house in Beverly Hills. We were Hollywood all right. And I did become a star, just not by my will. He released the movies of him and me in our most intimate and passionate moments all over the Internet. It gave me an incredibly bad image. To add insult to the injury, I had to find out about the whole thing being on the Internet from some pervert pastor.

Seriously, what was a pastor doing looking at that amateur porn site that my ex posted me on? I was devastated. Then, word had got around to my friends and that's when I was practically labeled as a no good whore. This label of being a no-good whore seemed to have stuck with me by both men and women since that video had caught fire on the Internet. And contrary to popular belief, just because a person may delete something from a certain page on the Internet doesn't mean that it's truly been deleted.

With the Internet, nothing is deleted and everything is fair game. I sent an email to the host of that amateur porn site after finding out about it. They took it down, but to my amazement, that filth showed up somewhere else. Not only did it show up somewhere else, but also somebody decided to narrate it, as if the sights and sounds of animalistic pleasure weren't enough narration to begin with.

Honestly, I don't know who I am anymore. Every day, I seem to lose one more piece of my soul, and I lose that much more control of myself. People around here be looking at me as if they know me. They judge me as if they know what I've been through.

Her tears had subsided, her loose baggy jeans felt much lighter as she forced herself to move half-heartedly with the music while she loosened up the pin holding her long Pocahontas like black hair. Alexis was often complimented for the richness and solid black texture of her hair, aside from her voluntary minor male like outer appearance; she kept herself well-groomed.

Some people even hate on me because I lust after the flesh of other women and my pent-up desires crave the silky-smooth bottom that was sculptured by the heavens for me to grab and hold on to. Unlike a sculpture, these desires are very real, and I can't help the way that I feel for a nice femme or maybe even a butch, too. Apparently, in this world, these types of desires make me different, maybe even less than a woman.

Pastors on the social networks have lied on me because I haven't been in their line for repentance. One pastor posted on my Facebook page that I was a child born for hell. When I saw that outrageous post and fifty people liked his comment, I shed enough tears that night to fill a small pond. First, what was he doing looking at my videos, and secondly, I thought that pastors were to encourage, not discourage people to seek after God. People like him can go to the bottomless pit and have my fried catfish sandwich ready for me when I get there. I don't even think that the gates of hell are wide enough to fit all the backsliding, trifling, money hungry, sex-crazed pastors that profess to be so— righteous in the eye of the public.

And my mother. Alexis looked on at the bypassing women; she licked her lips in the process, she hoped she could find an easy prey in the cover of darkness. *My mother, oh no, I don't even want to talk about my mother; my mother was a little loose back in her younger days. Let's just say that my mother specialized in lying on her back to pay the bills. Now she acts as if she doesn't even know me at times. Why? Because my mother found God and that's when she began to relish in her religious spirit. She hardly wants anything to do with me because of the choices I have made in my life.*

She acts like she's Miss Goody Two Shoes. She tried to act like she ain't never did something. Shoot, I heard that my mother was looser than two dogs in heat. I just feel like she needs to be more transparent with people, acting like she's such a holy roller. I know her dirty little secrets anyway.

No more lying, no more crying, no more creeping, no more sneaking. The truth, well— let's just say that the truth must be told. And if it's not apparent enough, the truth is this; I, Alexis Carter, am a fully converted lesbian.

She bowed her head, licked her lips, and moved with the rhythm of the music once more.

*****

Pain has been the name of my game ever since the college thing. My life had never been the same. Rats and roaches from back at the crib couldn't have prepared me for this because the people around these parts seem to be dirtier than the dirtiest, grimiest rodent. People are constantly judging me, trying to find a way to put me down. They try to make me feel like a fool, so what if I want to put my arms around my home girl. I got swag, and half of the dudes I run cross hate on my swag because I am pulling more girls than them. Just because celebrities like Ellen and Anderson are out, doesn't mean that I don't get weird stares when I show my affection in the open.

Ooh… look at that honey right there, "Yeah you swing those hips, dark chocolate. Come here and let me put some caramel on it." *That's just for giggles, she probably can't even hear a sister girl.*

Ooh… I discovered me a white girl. I love me some white girls, they form the best partnerships. She's a blonde. I definitely need to grow some and gone on over there and talk to her stilettos wearing, chest peculating, lips like Kool-Aid of a woman. Besides my evident attraction to white women, I can't help but see it as an added plus. The majority of them have good money, good credit, good family history, and well, everything else takes care of itself.

Tonight I am on a highly paid woman alert; I rolled up in Club S by myself, and I'd be crazy to be leaving the same way I came, so I am doing a full-blown scouting report. Unlike those punks down the street at Club G, we don't do any cross-dressing here at Club S.

Sodom is the exclusive club in Tallahassee for women only. Everyone is very discreet, and according to the many times that I've been here, you're bound to hook-up with a chick at least, seventy percent of the time that you come. That's a good statistic. They can do whatever they like at Gomorrah; we ladies don't have time for the drama I hear going on at Club G. Apparently the guys at Club G aren't good at being discreet.

I heard that the guys who are on the DL be giving the boys who are fully out a hard time. There ain't nothing more amusing than to see two punks fighting, and believe me, them boys be fighting worse than chicks, every other week I'd see one of their fights posted up on that world star website.

Girls around here be getting their haircut bald, and they still don't look like dudes, at least, not to me. She shook her head in laughter, as she thought about the many transformations she'd seen in just a few short weeks of attendance at the club. *I don't see the point in cutting my hair, unless I'm about to register for the military; I love to rock my long luscious hair. And the weave business is a little short without me because I rock all natural.*

"Oh my God, Oh my God." *There goes another fine white girl. She thick too. Maybe I should go talk to her, see if I could get that credit card number up off her, and maybe a few more digits while I'm at it. The girl looks like she has a bar tab for six people.*

Alexis lightly scurried her way over to the bar. All sense of humiliation, fear, and depression long left her. Her confidence level was a ten out of ten.

I might as well, make good use of my time here at Club S. It usually gets real live round here at about one in the morning, it's twelve thirty now, so it's time for me to go for the kill shot. She leaned over the bar; she sneaked over and seated herself next to the girl. Her stealth mode worked, she went unnoticed at first glance.

Hollering at a guy and trying to holler at a girl is very different. That's what I be trying to tell these dudes that just blatantly hate on me. Now, if the girl is a hardcore lesbian chick that typically cuts her hair low and is very aggressive, then she's a butch, and hollering at a butch is like hollering at a guy. But if the chick is more girly, a natural acting chick, then she's a femme. There are no laws that say that femme's and femme's can't be together or two butches either. I consider myself a cross between a butch and a femme.

I am a tougher female to figure out because I wouldn't dare cut my hair down like a butch, but I can be very aggressive while also retaining some of my basic feminine qualities.

This is the way I usually like to handle it, "Hey girlfriend, can you imagine anybody better sitting next to you because I can make a million dollars pleased to see you." *I said to the white girl, whom I will call chick number one for now, til' I get her name.*

"No, no one else is coming," chick number one quickly glanced to her left, and then she just as briskly went back to her shots.

"Oh okay, so you don't mind if I sit here next to you." *I'm trying to smooch the girl. So far, it doesn't seem as if it's working, maybe this chick has had a bad day, but she won't even look at me while I'm talking. She can't be straight, straight girls don't come to lesbian clubs. What's her deal?*

"No, I don't mind you sitting here at all," her head jerked back as she continued to rack up the liquor. *It must have been a tough day for this dime piece.*

"I actually came here by myself and am happy to have someone to talk to now. You know a fine woman is hard to find."

She threw me a wink. That's just the confirmation I needed, she's not straight, and she's open for business.

"So what's your name," I asked chick number one, barely hearing her response over J. Lo's new track blazing over the sound system.

After asking me to repeat myself three frustrating times, she finally said, "My name is Karen."

Karen and I shared a few laughs, and even talked a little about our lives. I don't believe she would have shared the stuff that she shared with me on just the first time meeting her if it wasn't for the liquor. We had some similarities in our struggles. Everybody has traumatic issues these days. I hope she wouldn't have an issue with me swiping her credit card numbers; I'm dying for me a new purse. All I need is a few prolific words, and then I'll be at her place of residence before the night is over.

Some girls say that I could be a dog, too aggressive and pushy. I'm nowhere near what some of these girls would do in this club just to score one for the night. I have seen chicks slipping pills in girls' drinks without their permission. I thought that those extremes were exclusive to guys, I guess not; at least, at Club S it happens all the time.

I ain't ever slipped one in a girl's drank, if she doesn't want to go home with me, then fine. I'll take one for the team and keep it moving. I'm too fine to be stressing over no chick. As my homeboy, Skip Blue likes to say, "There are way too many fish in the sea to get caught up slippin, pimpin." My homeboy is so— hilarious. That dude is the very definition of straight, he's smooth and, oh yeah, very attractive. If I weren't as fascinated about women as I've become, I'd probably try him out for loose change. Otherwise, I'm sticking to what I know, and what I know is sitting right next to me, all alone, ready for me to ask her out.

"So Karen, you got other plans for tonight, you know the night is still young, if you take down one more shot, girl, you'll be throwing up all over the club." Alexis paused. "Hey, why don't we go get some fresh air, talk about our problems, and you know, go from there?"

"Yeah, that sounds fun; I need to get out of here. Hey, what's your name?"

"I'm Alexis, but my friends call me Lexi. You can call me Lexi." She licked her lips with more desperation; she was excited about the promise of a good time for a few hours. A time when God's laws are broken, a moment which passion often overrides the guilt, Alexis was ready to sin again.

"Okay Lexi, where do you want to go first?" Karen slipped the bartender her card and left a cash tip on the table.

"Well… um… I was thinking my place. I have a nice 'lil' apartment with a balcony with the capitol building in view. I figured we can order out some wings or something." *I hope she takes the bait; the surge of feelings below my waist can't stand it anymore. I'm ready to have some fun.*

"Alright that's fine with me; at least, we don't have to pay a cover charge." Karen laughed.

Either this girl is that ditsy, or my game is just hot. It doesn't even matter now; I got her confirmation, now it's just time to get to second base because when I do, I know I'm scoring a home run.

"You ready." Karen asked a little light on her feet, a little tipsy too.

"Yeah, I'm ready. Let's go."

Ready set here I go, on to the new life in which I know. Lusting after women like a woman to a man, my life is indignant of God's plan. I love this life too much to turn back now, can't a man do what a woman can, her lips, her breast, her tender sweet touch, oh the thought of her all over me is just too much. I used to like that feeling. That touch of a man, but my ex-boyfriend ruined my opinion of all men. I'm dying to be straight, too; at least, that's what I tell myself. But my actions say another thing, maybe one day I will truly find myself. For now, Karen is the sheep and I am the wolf. I will devour her because my hormones have spoken.

Welcome to Club S, it's always a girls' night out here.

*Available **Now** wherever books are sold.*

Dying To Be Straight!

Take The Pledge (I WANT TO BE SET FREE!)

"For whosoever shall call upon the name of the Lord shall be saved."
-Romans 10:13 K.J.V.

Dear Lord God I struggle with this sin, this sin of homosexuality. Lord God I know that you are all powerful and an awesome God, so right now I lay down my life to you. I want you more now than ever. I don't want to be stuck in this lifestyle of homosexuality. Lord God I know that you are greater and you have so much more for me, it is through Jesus Christ that I will be delivered today and I will be set free!
So, I pledge to live a lifestyle of freedom from this day forward, so I can be a champion for Jesus Christ, living a Godly life. Free from homosexuality, free from my addictions. Amen.

Name:
_____

Date:
_____

If you have just taken this pledge then I must say congratulations. God is so good and he can deliver you from anything which you ask of him, there is no problem too big or small for God. Jesus died for every one of our sins including the sin of homosexuality; never feel like it's too late. I know you may struggle like Paul Stringer, but continue to press forward into Christ. Right now is the time to find a good bible based Christian Church if you don't already enjoy a church home. Take this pledge and place it in a secret place, this is between you and God. Then when you feel weak, remember this pledge and lean on God's word which is in the bible, his words precede anything else you could ever read or I could ever write. I love you my fellow brother or sister, but most importantly, God loves you most.

"That if you shall confess with your mouth the Lord Jesus and shall believe in your heart that God has raised Him from the dead, you shall be saved."
-Romans 10:9 K.J.V.

Did You Enjoy Reading Dying To Be Straight?
If so... Please write a review at any online retailer that carries this book. Be Blessed.

Made in the USA
Columbia, SC
22 June 2020